WITH EVERY BREATH

SASKIA WOODHILL

Lightpool Publishing

www.lightpoolpublishing.com

he second time Alba entered the huge, marble floored entrance foyer at the MoreIT in downtown Auckland, she wasted no time on admiring the gigantic aluminium angel's wings suspended from the ceiling three floors above her head. She was too busy concentrating on mentally sorting through what questions she might be asked in this second interview, because having been told she was one of two remaining candidates for the job she felt slightly pressured. Coming up with calm and self-possessed replies and sounding confident without being overconfident was the key, and those qualities were probably more important in this interview than in the first, so she had to get it right.

Getting this job with considerably higher pay than the one she had now would make a big difference for her and her father, so it was important to make a good impression. She had taken care to dress nicely and thought long and hard about how to do her hair. A topknot was out of the question, it made her look like a schoolgirl, and she had finally decided on a low ponytail, which she felt made her look tidy and hopefully adult and responsible enough for the job she had applied for.

As she rode up in the elevator and studied her reflection in the mirror clad walls she remembered her father's words on a previous occasion when she had moaned about how everyone thought she was a teenager. 'You'll be pleased about it ten years from now, so don't knock it,' he'd said. 'Your mother was exactly the same – people refused to believe she was a qualified accountant until she was at least thirty.'

But today she would have liked to look her age. Sometimes she could see that people didn't take her seriously because they thought she was fifteen or sixteen, and though it was mostly irritating there had been a few occasions when she had laughed inside at the expressions on someone's face when she came out with something they didn't expect from a teenager.

The small room on level five was not the one where the initial interview had taken place but a less formal room with four light armchairs arranged around an oval coffee table. In addition to Gregory whatever-his-name-was from the human resource department, who had conducted the first interview, there was also a severe looking, middle-aged woman dressed in a dark business suit and a white blouse in the room. Both stood up and shook hands, and the woman was introduced as Ms Winterdale, the head of the accounting team. To Alba's relief Ms Winterdale serious face was transformed when she smiled, and Alba smiled back in relief and sat down on the opposite side of the table from the other two.

'As you know already we aren't necessarily looking for people with a lot of specific experience,' said Gregory. 'Ms Winterdale thought it would be a good idea to get someone she can train herself instead of someone with previous experience with other software and other systems. We have systems here that are specific to the company, and we think the idea to kind of start from scratch and train someone from the ground up, might work out well. As I told you on the phone, you're one of only two remaining candidates. You were very evenly matched on the aptitude tests with nearly identical scores, so we thought we'd ask you back to find out a bit more about some of the qualities that might be useful in this position.'

'Thank you for asking me back,' said Alba politely and thought that probably their systems were designed in-house, so their approach to hiring seemed like a good idea.

A few minutes later, after answering some general and a few specific questions from Ms Winterdale, Alba got to her feet, desperately hoping that her face didn't reveal the frantic surge of feeling that had abruptly invaded her mind.

'Thank you,' she said and tried to sound calm despite her internal turmoil. 'I'm very sorry to have wasted your time, but I don't think this position is for me.'

Taken utterly by surprise the two on the other side of the table stared first at Alba, then at each other and had no time to say anything before she quickly left the room without another word, leaving total silence behind her.

'How did it go,' asked her father through the open back door when he came home from work that evening. As usual he peeled off his overalls and left them in the laundry room before he came into the kitchen. 'Did you get it?'

'I'll tell you about it after you've had a shower,' said Alba and turned from the chopping board, unwilling to start this conversation while he stood there in his boxer shorts, as always longing to get cleaned up after a hard day's work. 'It was weird, but let's not talk about it now – go and have your shower while I finish making dinner.'

She saw Steve's puzzled glance out of the corner of her eye, as she picked up one of the potatoes she had just scrubbed, but after hesitating for only a moment he disappeared down the passage to the bathroom and she smiled. He always knew when not to push things, or as her mother had once said, Steve was a man who knew how to wait. As always when she thought of her mother and the things they had talked about during the long months of her illness, things that were perhaps unusual for a mother and a daughter to discuss, Alba felt her heart clench with sadness.

Steve returned in jeans and a T-shirt and got a can of beer out of the fridge. Leaning a shoulder against the fridge he flicked the tear-tab and took a deep swallow before he lowered the can and looked expectantly at her.

'So, what happened? Something weird?'

She turned the heat down under the potato pot and said, 'I didn't stay for the whole interview. I was only in the room for a few minutes and then I got that panicky feeling, so I apologised for wasting their time and left right away.'

'A panicky feeling?' Her father looked concerned and stood up straight. 'Why? What did they say to you?'

'Oh, it wasn't anything they said. I got that feeling you get when you know someone near you poses a threat, and you just *have* to leave. You know - when it feels like your mind is shouting at you to get out fast,' said Alba, increasingly frustrated by the confused look on Steve's face. 'You know what I mean, that whatever-it's-called feeling - it must have a name, I suppose, but I've never talked about it before, so let's just call it the dread feeling.'

'I think we need to sit down and have a chat about this,' said Steve unexpectedly and opened the fridge again. 'You've still got some wine left in the bottle that's been sitting there for a week. I'll pour you a glass and we'll sit down so you can explain this dread thing to me, because I haven't got a clue what you're talking about. I can see it's important, so how about you tell me exactly what happened, right from the start – tell me every single thing that was said in that meeting.'

Very puzzled now and feeling slightly worried Alba wiped her hands and sat down at the table and tried to think what it could be that made him insist on talking about this. Did he think she should have gone through with the interview despite the dread feeling and maybe take the job anyway? Did he think she was showing a lack of strength in obeying that feeling and abandoning the interview?

'Right!' he said and put the wine glass in front of her. 'Now, would you please explain what the dread thing is and what they said, so I can understand how this happened.'

'Oh, for heaven's sake, dad! It wasn't anything they *said* – it isn't about what people say, is it? It's just that sensation in your mind. You know, that feeling you get when a person just fills you with dread and you know you must leave immediately, so that's what I did.'

'I've never had the dread feeling in my life,' said her father calmly. 'And I don't think I've ever heard of anyone else having it either. Not unless someone's made a threat or tried to intimidate someone, and you say that didn't happen. Has this dread thing happened before? And what if you don't leave, what happens then?'

Alba looked into his eyes, wanting to make sure he was serious, not just trying to make light of it to comfort her. 'You've not had that feeling – not ever?'

'I don't think so, not the way you describe it. I've found people scary sometimes. I got out of the way of an angry drunk once in a pub when I had feeling he was about to punch me, but I don't think that's what you're talking about, is it?'

'Oh no, this is a totally different thing,' she said and thought for a few moments while he watched her intently. 'This is so weird, dad. I thought everyone got that feeling sometimes. It's kind of like a warning, very urgent. It's only happened about three or four times in my life, but it makes me feel super stressed, like I've got to leave that very second and go somewhere else, as far away as possible, right away - it's terrifying. Each time it's happened I've just up and left, no hesitation.'

'What would happen if you didn't leave? Did you ever stay to find out?'

'God, no! I couldn't! It's the most compelling urge, it's like a voice yelling inside my head to get out, get away, leave immediately. And I have – so far, anyway. It makes me feel desperate. I've got no idea what would happen if I didn't leave.'

She thought for another minute and tried to define that impossible-to-ignore feeling. 'But you know what? I never thought of this before, but maybe I should have. It can't be a threat of something imminent, can it? I mean, in that meeting today – obviously nobody was going to attack me, so it must be that a person will be dangerous some time in the future in some way or another, perhaps not physical. I really don't know – it's just a compulsive urge to leave.'

Her father took another sip of his beer and studied her face for a moment before he said thoughtfully, 'So it's not what people call a panic attack – if it was then running away wouldn't solve it, so the dread feeling is a general warning to get away from a specific situation, is it?'

'Exactly! As soon as I leave the feeling stops and I feel normal again, relieved and calm.'

Steve had progressed from bewildered to clearly fascinated, said, 'Mary would have loved to hear about this, don't you think? She had that slightly mystic Korean inclination. A bit superstitious and far more accepting than I am of that kind of thing. Did you tell her about it when it happened before?'

'No, I've never thought of telling anyone.' Alba took a sip of wine and smiled at the thought of her mother. 'You're right about mum, though. She would have liked hearing about this. But it never occurred to me before right now that it isn't something everyone feels now and then. Or perhaps it's just you who don't feel it, perhaps everyone else does.'

When they were ready to go to bed that night, he pulled her close to his side with an arm over her shoulders. 'Follow your instincts, darling,' he said and kissed the top of her head, and she knew he meant it. 'Make sure you always get out of the way of that dread thing before it gets you. It sounds like a great early warning system to me. Evolution put the flight instinct in us for a purpose, for survival.'

Alba lay awake for a long time thinking about their conversation and about her mother, who despite her very factual and pragmatic mind had also believed in things that often made her father laugh, though not unkindly. 'Here we go again,' he'd say. 'A bit of Korean mysticism coming up.'

Before she went to sleep Alba went through every moment of the meeting at MoreIT and tried to pinpoint exactly what it was that had triggered that feeling. She had only realised when she talked to Steve that she hadn't mentioned it to anyone before, and she was surprised by the idea that maybe it wasn't something other people experienced. Or perhaps some did, but not Steve, and now she needed to analyse it and try to get a grip on it. Understanding it better suddenly felt important, something she had never even considered before, when she thought everyone felt it sometimes. Or rather, she told herself, she had never thought about it at all, but if someone had asked, she would have said exactly what she said to Steve.

She lay on her back, looking at the shadow of the plum tree silhouetted on her blind by the moonlight and went through what had been said in the interview immediately before she felt that strong urge to leave, but nothing particularly significant came to mind. And then she recalled to last time it had happened, and she knew she was right. The dread feeling was not caused by a look or a word or a threatening comment, or even someone looking at her directly, it was just a strong urge compelling her to leave immediately, but somehow she knew each time who had made her feel like that. It's directional, she whispered to herself, it's nearly got substance, and if I could see it I think it would be like a dark grey fog bank coming towards me very fast, rolling along the ground to swallow me up. From one person toward me. She tried to push the memory of the man on the bus out of her head, turned on her side and hoped she would be able to sleep without dreaming about him.

2

The following morning, as was their habit now that it was only the two of them, Steve got the breakfast things out while Alba showered. They sat opposite each other at the table with sunshine streaming in the window, reading news on their phones and hardly talking until Steve suddenly put his phone down and said, 'I'll be sixty-seven in June.'

Alba looked quizzically at him. 'And? Do you want a party - something special? We could have Morgan and the whole crew for dinner here or go out somewhere, perhaps? We haven't had anyone for dinner for ages.'

'It's not about doing something on my birthday,' he said, and now his expression was so serious that Alba put her phone down too and waited for what was coming with a slightly worried feeling creeping into her head.

'It's the mortgage. When I leave work I'll only

have the general pension and I know I'd not be able to keep up the payments to the bank.'

'Didn't you pay it off, ages ago? I think I remember mum telling me you were debt free a few years ago.'

He frowned down at his bowl of abandoned cereal. 'We paid the original mortgage off five years ago, yes – it had a twenty-year term - and then we decided that with Mary having such a well-paid job we'd take out another loan and do what she called retirement-proofing the house. Remember how we sat down together and decided how to renovate the bathroom and have a walk-in shower and new appliances in the laundry and the kitchen? And solar water heating.'

His eyes were not focused on her, he was remembering the discussions he and her mother had about what they would do, and Alba sat silent and waited.

'That's what we were planning to start with, and then we decided to do the whole upgrade thing, so we added a couple of things to the list, extra insulation and air conditioning, so when I retired and my income ceased, we had done all those expensive things. But Mary got ill …'

'And now you're worried about that mortgage and how long it will take to pay it off?'

'Yeah, because the worst thing is that I won't be able to continue working much longer now that my back's getting so much worse all the time. The doctor says when the sole of your foot has pins and needles all the time, quite apart from the pain down the leg, it's severe sciatica and the source of the problem is in my spine.'

He drank some coffee and Alba, silently studying him across the table, suddenly realised that his handsome face was far more lined than only a year ago and he finally looked his age. Was it the pain or grief?

'I didn't know about the pins and needles,' she said and felt guilty that she had never asked more than causal questions. 'You should have told me, dad! I suppose your work is very hard on the back, so it's only getting worse all the time and it never has time to recover.'

'Being a truck mechanic is heavy work, and I spend a lot of time kneeling or bending and lifting heavy parts. I've been thinking about it a lot lately, and I think we should sell this house and buy a flat, just two bedrooms and enough space for the two of us until you decide what to do next. Any day now you'll fall in love and move out, and what do I want with a house with three bedrooms and a big garden then?'

'But we love this house, and you love the garden, dad! It's your main hobby apart from the band - your dahlias and the vegetable garden.' She gestured at the window and the garden lit by morning sun. 'I can't imagine you living in a flat, it's just not you. I know what you're thinking, selling the house would give you enough money to pay the mortgage off and have a bit of retirement capital perhaps? Is that it?'

He nodded and drank the last of his coffee before he got up. 'That's right. Now that people subdivide and build what they call in-fill housing, this place has become valuable. Someone who knew how to subdivide and develop it could probably fit two additional houses on this site, maybe three. I talked to a guy at work, who has sold off the back part of his place, and he said a developer would pay a premium – what they got for the piece of land they sold surprised me. Way more than the mortgage I'm worried about.'

He drank some of his beer and put the glass down with a little bang. 'But you're right. Of course, I'd rather stay here now the house is so comfortable and needs nothing doing, but I've got to be realistic.'

'And you don't want to sell the back garden, or two thirds of it, and have a much smaller garden yourself so you can stay here?'

'I don't think I can.' He sounded slightly unsure 'It probably wouldn't work – not with the bank having this place as security for the loan.'

Alba thought for a moment. 'How much is left of the mortgage?'

'It started out at sixty thousand and it's still a bit over fifty. Not a fortune, but when I stop work I'll only have the pension to live on and that will make life difficult. If Mary had worked until retirement age, or even just ten years longer than she did, it wouldn't have been a problem, she earned so much more than I do.'

'I wish I hadn't walked out of that damn

interview yesterday! That job would have paid heaps more than I get at the warehouse. It was a selfish, stupid thing to do!'

'No, definitely not!' said Steve and reached for her bowl. 'You shouldn't go against an instinct as strong as that, no way! We'll talk about it later and decide together. There's no hurry. But isn't it ironic that we had my life insured because I was so much older, but not Mary's?'

All that day while Alba walked up and down the long aisles in the huge car parts warehouse, packing boxes, looking things up on her tablet and ticking things off on her clipboard, she tried to think of a solution. She would have to get a job that paid better, and going back to her studies was out of the question now. She needed to earn some serious money and help pay that mortgage off, not just help pay for the running costs at home. Or a second job, she thought as she pushed her large flat-deck trolley to another aisle and scanned the shelf for the part she needed. Another job in the weekends would work, perhaps something in a bar or a café. Not that the pay would be any better, but it would mean more money and it all added up until she found a job with higher pay.

She left the trolley where it was and went back to the central aisle, pushed the tall, wheeled ladder unit around the corner and engaged the wheel locks, still speculating about possible solutions.

Selling her mother's car was another source of ready money which could be a buffer zone for when things got tight. I've got to be sensible, and I don't really need a car, she told herself as she climbed to the fourth level shelf, it's quite new, so we would get a good price and it would save on registration and insurance costs as well. I can use dad's truck if I need a car, and I nearly always take the bus anyway.

The thought of her father living in a flat with either no garden, or just a tiny one, made it impossible to stop worrying about it, because she knew he would never be happy in a flat. Frustrated thoughts revolved in her head the whole day, but apart from taking a part-time job in the weekends of evenings, she could think of no practical way of making their situation better.

At the end of the day grey clouds scudded across the sky and the temperature was dropping. Mark was standing on the edge of the loading dock when Alba came out of the staff kitchen with her little lunch satchel. 'You'd better run fast today, Alba. I think it's going to rain - I can feel the air pressure dropping. Didn't you have a jacket hanging in the lunchroom?'

'I took it home yesterday - typical. And this morning was so gorgeous that I didn't even think of taking it, but getting wet won't do me any harm. See you tomorrow.'

By the time she got to the corner of Church Street she was soaked to the skin but running fast had kept he warm. Her thoughts were so focused on the mortgage and worry about her father that she nearly ran past number thirty-five and only realised where she was when loud barking brought her focus back to the present.

'Oh no!' she said to the large black Labrador who stood on his hind legs at the gate with his front paws on the top rail waiting for her. 'I'm sorry, big boy, I nearly missed you. What are you doing out in the rain? You're soaked.'

As usual she rubbed his ears while she talked to him for a few minutes, but standing still was fast cooling her down, so she told him to be a good boy and continued running through the rain which was now pelting down.

'For heaven's sake, darling!' said Steve when she stopped in the little hallway inside the back door. 'You're drenched! Didn't you take a jacket?'

'No, of course not, it was a perfect day when I left, and I hadn't checked the forecast.' She pulled the soaking sweatshirt over her head and tossed it on the floor in the laundry room, followed by her trainers and jeans. 'I'll sort that mess out in a moment, I'll just get into some dry clothes and get warmed up.'

After dinner when they were watching the TV news together Steve muted the sound and turned his head. 'What's that funny noise?' He made a move to get up, and Alba made a gesture to stop him. 'It's just my sneakers bumping around in the dryer with the stuff I took out of the washing machine.'

'You put your shoes in the dryer? I hope you cleaned them first.'

She reached across and patted his arm, 'Don't worry, Mr Fusspot! I scrubbed them in the tub and dried them a bit with an old towel, and they're in one of those mesh bags, so they won't touch anything else, but I need them for tomorrow. My proper running shoes aren't any good on the ladders.'

When Alba's phone signalled a call just before lunchtime a few days later, she looked at the unknown number and nearly didn't answer, but then she changed her mind. Better check who it is, she thought, and sat down on the edge of her trolley leaning against the bin of shredded paper they used for packaging.

'Hi Alba,' said a man's voice she didn't recognise. 'My name's Jake. I work at MoreIt. Have you got time to talk to me for a few minutes?'

'OK, it's just about time for my lunch break, so I can talk,' said Alba and wondered what this was about. Surely an employer wouldn't call to reprimand you for walking away from an interview, or would they?

'Is this about a job?' Her hopes rose immediately, only to fall flat when she realised she couldn't work for that company in any role at all.

'No, it's not, but I had a chat to our HR manager this morning, and he told me about the aborted interview the other day. Would you mind if I ask you a couple of questions? We're very intrigued.'

'OK,' said Alba and heard the reluctance in her voice even as she spoke. But being ungracious was no crime, and she didn't really want to talk to this man. She certainly wasn't going to tell him any details of why she had left so abruptly.

'Thank you,' he said politely. 'Who was it who said something in that interview that made you leave? And can you tell me what it was they said?'

'Who are you?' asked Alba instead of replying. 'I mean, what's your role?'

'Part of my role is acting as a glorified supervisor. I'm in charge of policy and a few other system things. If we don't have good procedures in place I need to know, so I can discuss it with others here and work out how we can improve what we do and how we do it.'

'Ah, well in that case I don't mind talking to you, but there was nothing in the interview that made me leave. I mean, not anything they said or implied. They were both perfectly polite, nothing upsetting was said at all.'

'That's what Gregory told me just now. He was baffled and so was Ms Winterdale. You agreed to come in for a second interview, spent five or ten minutes in the room and left without explanation. You can understand why it's important that we find out why.'

'Oh, please apologise to them from me,' said Alba, hoping this approach would put a lid on the issue. 'I *did* say I was sorry for wasting their time when I walked out on them like that, but perhaps you could tell them again, so they don't worry about it.'

'But *why* did you leave?'

She had known this was coming, the inevitable, simple question that she didn't want to answer. The dread feeling seemed deeply personal, and there was no way she could describe it to a stranger over the phone, not if it never happened to others, which she now knew was a possibility. If he hadn't heard about it before, he wouldn't believe her, but that thought gave her a sudden idea. Perhaps it would be worth telling him just a little, to hint at it. If he thought she was a bit crazy he'd probably stop asking questions and just write her off as not worth bothering with. She would try to give him the impression that she was a bit weird without going into any details.

'It was just a feeling I got,' she said airily, as if it was of no consequence, as if she regularly walked out of significant meetings and conversations for no particular reason apart from a vague feeling. She nearly laughed at the image this idea generated in her mind; how mad it would make her seem.

'What kind of feeling? Did they frighten you? Did you feel intimidated?'

'Not really, but it's hard to describe. I felt that I …' She couldn't continue because she had just been about to say too much and leave the way open for more probing questions. 'It's complicated,' she said instead and waited to hear what he would say next.

'OK,' he said patiently. 'But this feeling was strong enough to make you get up and leave. Can you describe it?'

'It was a strong kind of … vibe, unpleasant.'

'From whom? Could you tell?'

'From the accounting woman, definitely.'

There was a long moment of silence at the other end, and Alba got up and started walking back down the long, wide centre aisle towards the open loading bay where the staff kitchen was on one side. And suddenly she felt irritated by this waste of her half hour lunch break, talking about something she'd rather not discuss with a man she didn't know.'How did you get my number?' she asked abruptly.

'I got it from Gregory, so I could talk to you. I really need to understand if there's something wrong with our interview process. Can we meet?'

'No.'

'That's a very uncompromising no.'

'It's called the "*unconditional no*",' said Alba firmly. 'I learnt it from a policeman when I was eight. You might not know this, but when someone says *no* like that, with no qualifier or excuse attached, it's *supposed* to mean "this is the end of the conversation" – it leaves no room for negotiation or debate. Usually.'

To her surprise he chuckled. 'OK, I get it, but I

still want to find out more, I'm very curious. And I'd like to make sure you're OK.'

'There is no need for you to do that,' said Alba firmly. 'I'm perfectly fine, and I can look after myself. Did the HR guy show you my CV?'

'No, I just asked for your phone number, that's all, after I heard what happened in the interview. Are you sure we can't meet?'

'There is nothing more I can tell you. I can't explain it, so just stop hassling me, please.'

She ended the call and went into the staff kitchen to have her lunch.

3

The text from Blair arrived when Alba was trying to find a box of VW air filters that must have been misplaced when it arrived. She heard her phone's text message alert and ignored it while she tried to think of a logical but wrong place where one of the guys might had put it. Having failed to find it, she wolf-whistled and when nobody returned the call, she yelled 'Shane!' very loudly, her voice echoing through the vast space, because he was the only one who might know apart from Mark. 'Where are you?'

From way over to the left and a bit behind her she heard Shane's voice, but the reverberations made what he said unintelligible, so she headed down the central aisle and looked down each side aisle until she spotted him on top of a mobile scissor-lift in aisle P.

'There's a box I can't find,' she said, standing directly below him and tilting her head right back. 'I looked it up on my tablet just now and it was part of an order logged last month, it was delivered on Monday, but it's not where it should be. Did you put that delivery away?'

'Nope, it wasn't me!' said Shane and leaned on the platform rail high above her. 'I think it was Mole, and you know what he's like, gets distracted and wanders off. Check in the loading bay, in that recessed corner to the right where the roller door emergency chain is. I've found stuff there before that's got shoved aside and left behind.'

Alba found four boxes in the loading bay corner and spent twenty minutes with a trolley getting them to where they should be. It takes so much time when they do this, she thought, but maybe Mole gets bored, he's not the sharpest guy I know, so he might not have a system. Perhaps he just takes a random box, doesn't check if there's more stuff for that aisle and ends up moving ladders and wandering around endlessly until he gets bored, and then he goes off and does something else. But finally, she had the four boxes stacked were where they should be, she had found the air filter she needed and remembered to check her phone. *Dinner at our place Sat at six, don't bring anything, Carla is experimenting.* And Alba replied: *Lovely, can't wait to taste what she's making.*

At the end of the working day Alba came across Shane when she was ready to leave. 'Did you find it?' he asked as they went down the steps beside the loading platform.

'Yep, right where you said. He'd left four boxes there. I'll be checking that corner regularly now, but it's such an annoying thing to have to do. And Mole must have ticked it off as having been delivered *and* stored, or it wouldn't have been in the system.'

Shane unlocked his helmet from his motorbike and shook his head. 'He's got no focus, he's very unconcentrated - he's probably ADHD. Do you want a ride? Faster than the bus. You can wear my helmet.'

'I'd love to, but I promised my mum I'd never go on a motorbike,' said Alba straight-faced.

'You don't have to tell her, do you? You're a big girl now.' Shane grinned, and Alba looked serious and said, 'My mum's dead, and she said she'd come back and haunt me if I did, so I think I'd better not do it. I usually run home - it only takes about ten minutes.'

Walking home she smiled at the look on Shane's face when she trotted out her haunting excuse, it never failed. It had always worked before, but this was only the second time she had used it since her mother died, and it seemed more powerful now than it had before. Nobody felt comfortable challenging a promise to a dead mother, least of all one who would haunt her. The last time she'd used it was when the brother of an old school friend had tried to entice her to try a party drug a few months earlier.

'It stops them in their tracks, and they have no answer,' she said to the black Labrador at number thirty-five and rubbed behind his ears the way he particularly liked. 'They can't quite bring themselves to risk it, you see, even if they don't believe in ghosts, which of course you and I don't. And I think being half Asian, as they call it, helps too, don't you? Kind of makes it more believable.'

The truth was less specific than what she said to Shane, but it was such a useful tool and if her mother could hear her use it so effectively it would make her laugh. Years earlier, long before she was ill, her mother had said jokingly, 'Remember this, darling, and I mean *forever* – if you do something you know I would think was wrong, I'll come back and haunt you when I die.'

'So, it's perfect,' said Alba now to the dog. 'She couldn't have given me a better excuse to back out of things I don't want to do, the ones where the unconditional no doesn't work.' She bent forward and looked into his brown eyes, and he licked her wrist. 'But I must run now, so be a good boy until I see you tomorrow morning.'

She turned after a few steps and the big dog was still standing up against the gate looking at her, so she waved to him and saw his tail wagging.

On Saturday night, when Alba arrived at Blair and Carla's flat and rang the bell her friend Linley opened the door and grinned at Alba's surprise.

'Yeah, I know! We've never been invited to one of these experimental food evenings before, but I bumped into Carla in the supermarket the other day and she invited us. Come in! Everyone's busy talking and I was the only one who heard the bell.'

'It's always interesting,' said Alba. 'I've been twice before, and each time I've met different people. Remember Grunt from a year or two ahead of me at high school? He was here last time I came. I hadn't seen him in years.'

'Six guests today, but no Grunt and not anybody I've met before. Apart from locals there's an American they met on a walking track somewhere - he's the blond guy talking to Zac out on the balcony. I'll introduce you to him.'

'Hi Alba,' said the American called Ludo and looked Alba up and down in a way she couldn't quite define but wasn't sure she liked. 'Pleased to meet you. What an unusual name.'

'Ditto,' said Alba. 'Were you named after the game or was the game named after you?'

'Aha – a smart chick!' said Ludo and Linley moved closer to Alba and said coolly, 'She's very smart and rarely spares anybody.'

Alba wasn't quite sure what it was Linley had picked up about this guy to make her act so protective, so to lower the nearly palpable tension she laughed and said lightly, 'Pay no attention to her! I do sometimes spare someone if I feel they deserve it. Not often, but sometimes when I'm feeling charitable.'

Ludo turned back to Zac without responding and said, 'But that article was so exaggerated, don't you think? They guy who wrote it had a political agenda, like a lot of them do.'

Linley rolled her eyes and touched Alba's hand. 'Let's go and talk to someone else,' she said in a tone of voice that Alba thought would send an unmistakable message to Ludo about his lack of manners. 'We'll find someone more interesting to talk to.'

Just then Carla appeared with a tray of saucers, each one with a small portion of food. In the centre of the tray was a sign with the words "Spicy carrot salad". Like on previous food tasting evenings they were asked to fill in a little form when they returned the saucers to the breakfast counter in the kitchen and give a verdict on a scale from one to five for spiciness, texture and something Carla defined as "blandness".

Linley wrote "spicy carrots" at the top of a form and turned to Alba with the pen poised and said, 'Blandness? You've done this before. What exactly does she mean? Like boring?'

Alba put her own form in the basket beside her. 'I think of it as uninteresting – what we used to call blah when we were at school. Remember those sandwiches with slices of hardboiled egg you used to have in your lunchbox?'

'Right!' said Linley. 'They were totally blah. My mom made the worst sandwiches, didn't she? Never thought of salt and pepper, and you got all those gorgeous Korean things. I think it was the reason we became friends, so I could share your lunch.'

When the second tray came around with a sign that said, "Cacio e pepe pasta (pasta with pecorino Romano cheese and black pepper)", Ludo appeared beside Alba. He picked up a bowl and said without any preamble, 'I'm sorry I was rude earlier. Do you think we could start again?'

'Of course,' said Alba and took a little bowl of pasta from the tray. 'Why are you in New Zealand? Is it a tourist trip or are you working here?'

'I'm doing a post-grad year at university here, towards a master's degree in wetland ecology that I'll complete back home.'

At the end of the evening, when six potential new additions to the lunch menu at Carla's café had been tried and evaluated, Ludo asked if he could have Alba's phone number. 'I haven't made many friends here yet,' he said with disarming honesty. 'I'm a bit of a nerd and I don't find it easy to make friends. Maybe we can get together sometime for a meal or something?'

4

On a Friday night a few weeks after the initial call, Jake called again. Alba looked at the screen, recognised the number and answered after first hesitating, but curiosity won. What could he possibly want now, after all this time?

'Hi, it's Jake again. I know you don't want to talk to me, but I think we must meet. And no, *don't* say it, please! I know you're just about to give me that unconditional no of yours, but could you hold it back until you hear what's happened?'

'OK,' said Alba politely. 'Something happened?'

'I discussed what you told me with a couple of senior people in the company – that it was Ms Winterdale who gave you that strange feeling that made you leave. Nobody had ever heard of anyone walking out in the middle of an interview, particularly not when they're one of the final two competing for a good job. But despite not having much to go on, we started a process. Did you look at the Stuff website any time after half past five tonight?'

'No.'

'Can you check it out now, please? I'll hold on, or you can call me back. Find the headline saying that *MoreIT calls in the auditors.*'

'OK, I'll call you back.'

Alba opened the Stuff app and scrolled down the headlines and there it was, fourth from the top.

'More IT, a major tech company listed on the stock exchange and well-known to many after impressive growth and expansion, from a start-up in a student bedroom twenty years ago and now on the global market, has issued a media release as follows: Due to apparent irregularities we have asked for a forensic audit of all our financial records going back three years. The Stock Exchange has been informed and our shares will continue to trade. Despite the possibility of fraud having been committed, the company's profits have always been substantial and shareholder dividends have been generous, as they will be again at the end of this financial year. No further information will be made public until the investigation has been completed.'

'Hi Jake,' said Alba without ceremony when he took her call. 'Do you think it's Ms Winter-whatever her name is?'

'Will you promise to keep this totally to yourself

if I tell you? I don't know if you're familiar with how the stock exchange works, but no specific details of this must get out until news about a prosecution is made public or they might stop our shares trading.'

'I know how it works, and I can keep my mouth shut, but I'd like to be able to tell my dad because I tell him everything. He's super-safe, they named Fort Knox after him. He makes oysters seem garrulous.'

There was that chuckle again, and Alba smiled.

'Nice word! Yeah, it's her all right,' said Jake. 'Which is why I must talk to you face to face. However you picked it up, that vibe you got from her was spot on.'

'How do you know it's her if you've just called in the auditors? Has she told you already?'

'We actually called in the auditors nearly a month ago, just after we talked the first time. We did a data crunch from our banking and accounting systems and the server audit trail, so from there it was perfectly clear. We only got the auditors in to sign off on what we found – to satisfy the cops and the stock exchange. Quite apart from anything else the internal audit trail on the server confirmed that everything we found was done from her logon.'

'I'd love to know how that works. The data crunching, I mean.'

'So, you'll agree to meet me? Just once, so I can ask some questions and I'll also explain how we did the data crunch. And by the way, what's your surname? I forgot to ask Gregory.'

'Asher,' she said. 'Alba Asher. My mum was hoping I'd become a film star.'

While she spoke, she'd been considering the pros and cons of meeting him. His motivation for telling her so much was based on his curiosity about the strong dread feeling she had got from Ms Winterdale in the meeting, though he didn't know it was dread, or what dread was. He just thought she had got an unpleasant vibe from Ms Winterdale. And though she didn't really want to talk about it again, the chance of finding out how a company as big as MoreIT ran an internal investigation in a situation like this was irresistible. An opportunity to get this kind of inside information might never come her way again, and it made a trade-off seem reasonable.

'OK, I'm not working tomorrow. Where do you want to meet?'

They made the arrangements and Alba leaned back in her armchair and stared unseeingly at the TV she had muted when she took his call. She thought of the many questions she wanted to ask the next day and the things she must work out about him as a person before she decided if she could trust him and tell him the truth. When Steve came home after his fortnightly band practise she only said she was meeting a friend the next morning and might not be home until the afternoon.

. . .

At ten minutes past eleven the next morning Alba was getting very hot and wished the café was on the shady side of the street, and nearly gave up waiting. He said eleven sharp, she thought and looked up and down the street again, and I told him I'd be wearing a pink top and wait outside, so I can't take my sweatshirt off. I assumed he's very punctual seeing he used that "sharp" expression, but maybe he's been held up. Though if that's the case he could have called.

An auburn-haired man, who had stood outside until a couple of minutes earlier and then gone into the café, came out again and stopped in front of her.

'Are you Alba?' he said, his tone incredulous, and she nodded.

'I've just had a look inside and then I noticed you're still standing there looking around – and you're wearing a pink top. My mistake, I wasn't expecting someone so … come on, let's go in and order.'

'What did you mean, you didn't expect someone so – what?' she said while they waited to place their order. 'Did you expect me to dress up?'

'I didn't expect a school leaver, that's all.' He shook his head and smiled. 'That's why I didn't think it could be you earlier when we were both standing outside. I thought if you'd been considered for that new role in the accounting department you'd be in your twenties at least with some work experience, not just out of school.'

'Sorry,' said Alba and turned to look at the cakes in the cabinet beside her to hide how close she was to laughing. 'I'm quite clever, you know.'

'Clearly!' was all he said, and then it was their turn to order.

Once they were installed at a table and their coffee had been delivered, Jake said, as if he was laying down the rules in a meeting. 'I've got a couple of things to ask first, and then I'll tell you about the data crunching and you can ask as many questions as you like.'

Alba nodded. This seemed like a fair trade; he was entrusting her with some sensitive information, so she must be prepared to tell him whatever he wanted to know. It would be interesting to see how this would turn out. She didn't know anyone in his particular age group; much older than her friends and much younger than her father, and he worked for a huge and well-known company. The possibility of learning useful things was exciting, and she smiled at the thought that in exchange for telling him what he was so keen to know, she should be able to ask nearly anything. The balance was heavily in her favour, and she intended to use it.

'Could you explain exactly what it was you felt - that vibe you got from Winterdale in the interview? Was it fear? I mean, did it make you feel frightened?'

Alba took a moment to consider how best to explain the concept of dread, which was far from clear in her own mind, but somehow she must convey what it felt like when it happened. Looking absently over his shoulder at the line of people waiting to order, she discarded one explanation after another. Nothing seemed to exactly describe what it was she had experienced, not in a way that would make sense to someone else. She didn't want to go through all the back-and-forth as she had with Steve to make him understand; she would prefer simply to tell Jake in detail and hear what he said.

Finally, after a lengthy silence while he waited patiently, she said, 'I know I said it was like an unpleasant vibe, but it's actually much stronger than that. And it's not like fear, not really. In my mind there's a big difference between fear and dread, the feeling I call dread - for want of a better word to describe it. Until it happened during that interview I'd never needed to find a word for it, it was just "that feeling". I had never talked about it with anyone until I told my father after the interview, though it's happened a couple of times before.'

She paused and drank some coffee to give herself time to think. 'To me, fear means something more immediate or defined, like you know what you're afraid of. This dread feeling is different. It's a very strong, undefined sensation of evil or danger, or maybe threat, but it's not specific, not as to what it's about – well, not apart from the fact that I can tell who it emanates from.'

She looked at him for a response, but he just waited, still silent and without expression. He doesn't understand it, she thought, so he doesn't believe me, and there's not much more I can say to describe it. It's too way out and it sounds so crazy, but I've got to finish now, as much for my sake as for his because I need to get this clear in my mind.

'When it happens I don't know if whatever that person is planning, or is capable of, or has done, is directed at me or involves me. Well, before that interview I *did* think it was always directed at me when it happened, and that's why I felt it at all. But seeing that Ms what's-her-name had committed fraud, perhaps the dread feeling I got from her just related to something bad, like a general badness thing. Oh no, wait! Maybe she was considering *me* in the context of what she had done, so it did involve me after all?'

She paused again and considered this idea. 'Yeah, that could be it, couldn't it? Maybe the dread feeling wasn't just about dishonest things she had done, but she might have been wondering if I'd be likely to discover something. You know, she might have been trying to work out what kind of person I am, and if she'd be able to explain it away if I came across something she had done and asked her about it. She wouldn't want anyone too smart or inquisitive, would she? But it's all guesswork – I really don't know what triggered it.'

'But you felt it so strongly that you just got up

and left, so it must have given you a feeling there was some level of potential harm for you.'

Alba had never before analysed the dread feeling in such detail but understanding it better might be useful in the future, so she was prepared to answer his questions. Maybe he would come up with something she hadn't thought of yet.

'No, not necessarily harm directed *at* me,' she said slowly. 'When I opted out of the interview I felt that she was dangerous and bad, and that I must protect myself by having nothing to do with her, not even staying in the same room. Not that I thought of it in such detail just then, I just felt it very strongly. You said that perhaps it was something that would be potentially harmful for me, and that's exactly what I meant before when I said she could have been considering how to deal with me, if I discovered something.'

'No,' said Jake slowly. 'I wasn't only meaning that. I wondered if she was playing out some scenario in her mind – something that had just occurred to her while you were talking. Which could explain why something suddenly gave you that feeling when it hadn't been there from the start. Perhaps she was working out if she'd be able to implicate you in some additional piece of fraud she was planning. Use you to deflect blame if it was discovered some time in the future. So, a real threat against you personally, which you picked up on, and which gave you that dread feeling.'

She could tell he was concerned about what he

had said and how she might take it. It didn't come across in his voice or from his expression, but she felt it strongly, like a warm touch on her skin. He's a kind man, she thought, he cares about people.

'You might be right,' said Alba after thinking for a moment. 'It *was* such a strong feeling, and it came on suddenly – and as you said, it wasn't there to start with, or I would have left before the interview even began. When it's happened before, I've never actually worked out if it's general evilness or not. It's only happened a couple of times before, three I think, but that time with the man on the bus …' Her voice tapered off into silence as she thought back to the bus experience that had left a trauma that was still alive like an active threat to her safety within her.

'The man on the bus?' he asked, curious now. 'Can you tell me about that?'

'No, I don't want to talk about it now,' she said firmly and wished she hadn't brought it up. It still had the power to make her tremble, and she needed to draw a line in the sand, make sure he understood there were things she might not want to share, however helpful it was to have this discussion with him.

'So, do you believe me, or do you think I'm exaggerating or just making it up?' She didn't need to ask, she knew he believed her, she could feel it, but she wanted to hear how he would put it.

'I think you have some kind of talent, like a litmus test for evil intent, let's say, though it sounds so dramatic I can't believe I just said it.' He smiled and she couldn't help smiling back. 'And I'd like to offer you a job.'

'The one I applied for? Didn't the other applicant take it?'

'No, not a job at the company office or even in the company building – let's call it an invisible job. I'll pay you a salary, you can have another job as well if you want to, but you would be on stand-by for me for when I need you.'

She couldn't believe she hadn't picked this up, that he could have hidden it so well, it was incredible. She shot a hard look at him that made him flinch.

'Oh, for God's sake, is that what this is about?' she said, her voice cutting through the air between them like a knife. 'Go and find yourself a whore somewhere else!'

She was about to get to her feet and leave, but he reached across the table and grabbed her wrist, and suddenly he was laughing which stopped her in her tracks.

'No, no! Please don't go, it's not about sex, calm down! I mean, you could be of help when I meet with investors and particularly when people want me to get involved with mergers or start-up proposals. Your kind of perception could be invaluable, and you'd be legitimately employed as a consultant – you'd be an asset to me.'

Alba pried his fingers from her wrist and sat back again. 'Are you kidding? You'd pay me for doing practically nothing?' She looked hard at him, serious and focused now. 'No strings attached at all?'

'I swear,' he said, and she could tell he really wanted her to believe him. 'On my honour, such as it is, there's nothing shady about this. I might need you to come with me to a meeting now and then or be there when I have a drink with someone and then tell me if you get the dread feeling. That's all, I promise. Let's say you'd be my truth filter.'

And then suddenly it struck her, the discrepancy between this offer and what he had originally told her what his position was when he made that first phone call weeks ago, and she knew he was a liar after all, which was confusing; she would normally have known right away.

'So, this kind of supervisor you're supposed to be, just overseeing various aspects of policy, I think you said – that's a role where you discuss mergers and hire invisible employees?' she said scornfully. 'Do you think I'm stupid?'

She made a move to push her chair back, and once again his hand clamped down on her wrist and anchored it to the table. 'Hang on! Let me explain, please.'

Still holding her wrist firmly with his left hand, he quickly logged on to the phone beside his coffee cup and tapped out a few words, waited a moment and slid the phone across the table. Alba knew what she would see before she looked down at the screen, she had understood in a heartbeat, and in her mind thoughts whirled like autumn leaves in a wind. Why had he not told her from the start? Was his offer genuine? Should she take him up on it and maybe be able to help her father?

Jake said nothing, just watched her face and waited until she looked up. 'If I hadn't threatened to leave, would you have told me?'

He let go of her wrist and she suddenly felt as if the air pressure had changed. Wow, she thought, so that intense feeling when he grabbed hold of me the first time wasn't something I imagined, it happened again. I wonder what it is. I feel things more strongly from this guy than from anyone I've ever met. I've got to be careful, it's as if I have a direct link to him somehow.

Through these brief thoughts Jake's eyes hadn't left her face, and now he said, 'Of course, I would have told you. You'd have understood it as soon as you sat in on the first meeting I took you to.' The corner of his mouth tweaked up. 'Does it make a difference?'

'Don't be silly! Of course, it makes a difference. I mean, if you're the CEO of the company, then your offer seems nearly realistic. Before, it was just too ridiculous to even consider, don't you think?'

Now he smiled and once again she just had to smile back. 'Quite right! I'd forgotten what I said my job was in that phone call. I only said that because I wanted to seem less threatening, I suppose, less important. So, you'd talk to me honestly.'

'Don't people talk honestly to you if they know who you are?' She got a feeling that he had told her something deeply personal, it was there in some hidden layer of his voice, she had felt his hesitation. 'Why would people lie to you?'

'I don't think they lie to me any more than they do to most other people. But sometimes they might want to impress me, make me take note of their venture, perhaps they overstate things to get what they want from me.' He sighed. 'Or they hope the connection will be useful, or they want a job or whatever. I don't know, it probably varies, but I often get a feeling that new people I meet are thinking on two levels while they talk to me – they see me as potentially useful.'

'Like you do with me.'

'Yes, but I'm being honest about it.'

'True,' she said and decided there were things she could tell me him now, things she hadn't been prepared to reveal earlier. Not because he was powerful or wealthy or whatever he might be, but simply because she believed him now, and she got a strong vibe that he was being honest and frank. He had told her the truth and he trusted her, and now she was prepared to trust him.

He looked at his phone. 'Have you got time for lunch? It's just after midday now – I just need to keep the office informed about how long I might be.'

'OK, I don't have to leave quite yet.' Deliberately

she left it open so she could leave on a made-up excuse if the need arose.

Jake 's conversation with someone who was probably his secretary, was brief and factual. 'Hi Elizabeth - I'm in a meeting, but I'll be back in time for the catch-up with Carl at three. Just text or call if you need to tell me anything. This is an informal meeting, so don't hesitate, I'll keep an eye on my phone.'

'Do you work on Saturdays?' she asked. 'And your secretary too?'

'At the moment we do. Think of what's going on - we've got to stay on top of this. Carl is the PR guy who's orchestrating our media responses. They've been trying to get comments from me since last night, and we'll probably need to make another statement to hold them at bay, give them a tiny bit more. It's important to not give the impression we're hiding anything – that there might be more bad news to come. It's exactly how much to give them that we need to discuss. Even a few words too many could have repercussions.'

'How old are you?' The question slipped out before she could stop herself. He was fit and strong looking, and he had thick brownish-red hair, but there was a sort of presence about him like an aura of strength, and she thought he might well be older than he looked. He was in a powerful position after all, and she wanted to know.

'Forty-three in August,' he said, unperturbed by this sudden personal interest, but she knew he was amused, she'd noticed the little twitch at the corner of his mouth. I'm right, she thought, there's a man who likes to laugh behind this serious, controlled exterior - maybe I can winkle his inner self out in the open. I feel it very strongly when he's enjoying something I say.

'And how old are you?'

'Twenty-five in November,' she said coolly with a straight face and watched with hidden glee as his expression changed to outright surprise. 'Yeah, I know. You thought I was eighteen, didn't you? Everybody does.'

'God no, seventeen at the most - more likely sixteen.' He shook his head. 'You look like a child. No wonder you're so stroppy and self-assured. Shall we order lunch now?'

'Can we go somewhere else? I'd rather not stay here.'

'Not dread again?'

'Oh God, no! If it was dread I'd be running full speed down the street right now, but I need to pee and I noticed the toilets here are uni-sex and I don't use those. One bad experience and you stay clear of them forever.'

'OK, of course – where do you want to go? How about the steakhouse down the street?' He got to his feet and waited for her to pick up the sweatshirt she had peeled off before she sat down. 'Or somewhere else where you feel happy about the toilets?'

'There's a nice sushi place I went to once, it's just a couple of blocks from here - if you don't mind. I love really good sushi, of course. And they have separate toilets there.'

'You should put your sweatshirt on before we go outside,' he said surprisingly. 'It's clouded over, and you won't be warm enough in just a T-shirt.'

5

They walked in silence to the sushi restaurant, occasionally getting separated by people going in the opposite direction, and Alba noticed that Jake kept a sideways eye on her whenever this happened. What was he expecting, she wondered, did he think she might run away? His expression, when she noticed him glancing over to see where she was, told her nothing, but she sensed his attention like a repeated light touch on her shoulder. This was a new sensation, something to add to the many feelings and hidden emotions she picked up so easily from others, and it intrigued her. It wasn't something she had come across before, so she deliberately went to the right around a man standing still looking at his phone, though she could easily have gone around him to the left, the same side as Jake. Yes, she was right, that glance in her direction was just like a touch, like a finger lightly making contact with her left shoulder. Like when she felt he cared about what he was telling her in case she got upset, the same kind of feeling of warmth. If it had a colour it would be a warm, pale yellow, she thought, like sunlight very early in the morning.

As soon as they got to the restaurant Alba went straight to the restroom and sat in a cubicle checking things on her phone. Jake Tobin was not only the CEO of MoreIT, but he was also the biggest single shareholder and had built the company from scratch, starting out twenty-two years earlier with money borrowed from his uncle. She scrolled through a few articles, saw photos of him with famous or important people at various events and decided he was exactly what he said, just as her intuition had told her. But from establishing the truth of who and what he was, to whether she would accept that strange job offer was a big step. She washed her hands, tucked a stray tendril of hair behind her ear and joined him at the counter.

'Tell me about yourself,' said Jake when they had selected sushi and were once again sitting opposite each other. 'I'd like to know a bit more, just the ordinary stuff. You know, family, background, that sort of thing.'

'Very average compared to you, not very interesting,' said Alba and put her chopsticks down. No way could she eat sushi and try to talk with her mouth full in front of anyone else but her dad; this wasn't Korea where it was all right to stuff a whole sushi roll into your mouth and continue talking. On an impulse she decided to give him the full disclosure at once, all the details, to avoid lots of follow-up questions, because this was clearly a man who asked questions all the time.

'I live in Church Street in Onehunga with my dad, my mother is dead, and I work in a warehouse, packing car parts into boxes. I have no siblings. I like walking in the bush, and I read a lot and I like cooking. Sometimes I have an exciting day when I get to ride right up to the top on the scissor lift unit - you stand on the platform as it goes up, way up. We've got big ladder units on wheels with platforms too, but they're not as exciting.'

'So, you don't mind heights?' Jake smiled, and she sensed amusement again not just polite interest. 'I'm very anti heights, particularly ladders.'

On an impulse she decided to tell him about the ladders. Not that there was any reason to, but she thought he might like hearing about them, and she enjoyed that feeling she got when she told him things.

'No, I don't mind heights at all, and the scissor lift's my favourite thing at the moment. But the mobile climbing ladders are fun too, you can push them along and stand on the cross-bar at the base and go for a ride right down an aisle, but you've got to be ready to put your foot on the wheel-lock pedal in case you nearly hit something, you can't really steer them. They're called Warthog – that's the manufacturer's official name for that model.'

'Are they as high as the ones they use in the

supermarkets to reach the stuff they stack on top of the shelves?'

'*Much* bigger, truly industrial size, and the scissor lift goes even higher, right up under the roof, very high. It's what we mostly use to put big boxes of parts up the top, extra supplies that we can restock the shelves with. We load up the platform and ride around doing it. Well, it's usually the guys who do the lifting. I can't lift the heavy boxes when they're full of stuff.'

'Where is the warehouse? Is it close to where you live?'

'It's in Penrose, close enough so I can run there in ten minutes. Perfect!'

'How did you know about the stock exchange? Do you speculate in shares?'

Alba got the giggles in the middle of a mouthful of sushi, which she had just put in her mouth without thinking and held her hand up like someone directing traffic until she'd finished chewing.

'Of course not! I don't have the money for that sort of thing. And don't you *ever* stop asking questions? You're like the elephant's child, and you know what happened to him.'

'No, I don't know what happened to him. You'll have to tell me.'

There was that held-back smile again, that little signal of secret amusement he probably had no idea she could sense. Even if she hadn't seen it, she would have known. She felt more strongly with every sentence they exchanged that she knew this man, that she had known him for a long time, and they understood each other on a level that didn't need words. She knew when he was amused or hesitated, as if there were some kind of stronger invisible link between them than what normally made her able to understand what people were hiding. It was confusing but also interesting, and on an impulse she decided to check out her instinct right then, though if she was wrong and he got angry this might be the end of things.

'OK, Mr Ignoramus,' she said using her bossy voice. 'This is how it was according to Mr Kipling, who you might have heard about. The elephants lived in the jungle by the great, grey-green, greasy Limpopo River, and the elephant's child asked questions *all* the time of *everyone*. He drove the other animals crazy. This was before elephants had trunks, they just had noses a bit like a cow or something - like this.'

She made a round snout-shape with her hands in front of her face. 'And then one day a grumpy old crocodile got really fed up with all the questions about what he had had for dinner, so he grabbed the little elephant's nose to pull him into the river, and the little elephant braked as hard as he could, and some other animals, I think it was a monkey and a snake, came to help him, but the crocodile pulled so hard that the elephant's nose got stretched out and became a trunk - and that's why elephants have trunks. But he didn't end up in the river.'

While she was telling the story, Jake's face had changed from interested to fascinated, and now he took a long drink of his green tea and said, 'Will you promise me something?'

'Depends on what it is. You tell me first and then I'll decide.'

'Promise you'll never change.'

She stared at him in surprise, her mind a blank. What on earth was he talking about? But he didn't look away or even blink, he just looked steadily back, so she said, 'OK then, Mr Boss-person. I promise I won't change.'

And then he surprised her. 'What happened once in a uni-sex toilet?'

Alba laughed. 'You're *definitely* closely related to the elephant's child! But OK, if you really want to know, this is how it was. I was sitting on the toilet, and I noticed a phone on the floor beside me that someone was pushing a bit further in. He was using his fingers to push it under the separating wall – you know how the walls between the stalls sometimes have a gap under them, so they're a bit off the floor. Maybe it's so they can hose the floors down? It was a man's hand - hairy knuckles.'

'What did you do?'

'I got up fast and stomped on the phone, smashed it. I was wearing my Doc Marten boots, so it worked really well.' She got the giggles thinking of it. 'And then that idiot in the next cubicle put his hand further in to pull the phone back, so I stomped on his fingers too. And then I pulled my jeans up and ran like crazy.'

'You've got great presence of mind! I'm *very* impressed,' said Jake and got up. 'I've got to go now, but I'll be in touch.'

When they parted outside, Alba turned down his offer to pay for a taxi. 'For God's sake, are you crazy? A taxi to Onehunga? I'll just catch the bus from the stop at Wellesley Street. Bye!'

She ran off and didn't look back and never saw Jake stand watching her until she disappeared around a corner.

6

When Alba messaged Jake on the Monday and said she would accept the contract position, he asked for them to meet the next day. She was surprised that he suggested meeting at the café at the shopping centre a few hundred metres from where she lived. Why was he prepared to come all the way out there? But she had a feeling she might be able to get more out of him by asking when they were face-to-face rather than in a text, so she just said yes, she would meet him there.

She was still intrigued with her discovery from their first meeting that she could pick up all kinds of things from him so clearly, much better than she usually could. Whether she watched his face or just listened to his voice, she felt his hidden amusement, knew when he was holding something back or even his slight hesitation when he revealed something personal, as he had once. The way she could read him so easily was the reason she knew she could trust him. She hadn't felt him lie even once, though she had accused him of it, when she thought she had missed a cue, but she had been wrong.

I'll ask him now, she thought the next day, as she stood waiting outside the café, scrolling through headlines on her phone, because he really took me by surprise when he suggested meeting here. Then she jumped when his voice came from right behind her. 'Ready for coffee?'

She swung around and found herself far too close to him and took a step back. 'You shouldn't sneak up on people like that! You could have given me a heart attack. Do you know CPR?'

'Nonsense,' he said briskly and held the door open. 'Are you coming? How long before you have to be back at work? I hope this isn't causing difficulties for you on a weekday. I didn't think of that until I'd already suggested this, and you'd agreed.'

Alba had never been inside this café, though she often went past it, and she was interested to see how much nicer it was inside than she would have expected from the exterior, and how much bigger. The walls were painted in soft greyish blue and there were bunches of dried flowers suspended in the corners, all the colours were muted and subtle which seemed to inspire a feeling of calm. They sat at a table in the corner by the window, and she looked around again, and suddenly realised she hadn't replied.

'Sorry, I got distracted by the colours on the walls, it's nice in here. I've never been here before. But it's OK for me to take a couple of hours off. I've got a lovely boss, and I promised I'll come in on Saturday to make up the time if he needs me. We only close properly on Sundays, we use Saturdays to catch up.'

'So, Bletchley's is a good place to work?'

Calm and deliberate, she delayed replying and looked steadily at him for a long moment. 'How do you know where I work?'

He raised his eyebrows at the implied suspicion. 'Last time we met you told me about the car parts warehouse, so I looked it up. There are only two places like that in Penrose, so I guessed it was Bletchley's because it's close enough for you to run to in ten minutes. Did you think I'd asked to see your CV?'

'Oh no, I'm sorry! That was rude. And there's no reason you couldn't look at my CV. Not that it's an excuse, but I didn't sleep well last night. Hardly at all, so I'm a bit frayed around the edges today.'

He frowned and looked searchingly at her. 'Why didn't you sleep? Are you regretting saying you'll accept the job?'

'Oh, no, not at all.' Briefly she considered making something up, but perhaps honesty would make him understand that she had a genuine reason to feel tired and out of sorts.

'Exactly a year ago today my mother died,' she said bluntly and looked down at her hands. Even saying the words made tears pool in her eyes and for some reason she didn't quite understand, she added a detail that only she and her father knew. 'I was alone with her when she died. I'd been her caregiver for the last year of her illness, so she wouldn't have to be in a care home or at the hospice.'

'That's hard – I'm sorry I asked to meet you today. You could have told me to wait.'

And then she thought how ungracious and difficult she was being and raised her eyes to his and blinked back the tears. 'Oh, please, no – it's not your fault! I'm just tired and grumpy. Please don't apologise! I was looking forward to this.'

'But? What is it you're not saying?'

She gave him a wry smile. 'I feel worried about your offer, about what you think I'll be able to do for you. It feels as if I'm holding out a promise that I might not be able to live up to. It's such a vague thing, isn't it - this dread thing, and I don't have any control over it, it just happens. What if I can't help you? If it doesn't work? But I promise I'll just abandon the contract if it doesn't work out. I mean if I can't sense a threat when it's directed at you, which I feel very doubtful about. I'm not about to take advantage.'

'That's not your problem, it's mine. And I'm not expecting anything, Alba. If you never get the dread feeling when I've asked you to sit in on something, that's OK. It might mean nobody's got any dangerous designs on me or the company, which would be great, but it could take years for your talent to give results, if ever – who knows? And I'm fully aware that the dread feeling might not apply if the danger isn't directed at you personally, so I could be on a wild goose chase, but I don't mind. The experiment is worth it.'

And straight into her mind flashed an idea that she couldn't believe she hadn't thought of earlier, and she felt a smile forming. He noticed, of course, and when she didn't say anything he gave her a searching look. 'That smile just now. Was it the prospect of being paid to do nothing much or something else?'

'Does it matter?' she asked cheekily, suddenly feeling upbeat and confident again. 'Will you sack me if I smile too much?'

'No, I just wondered what made you smile, but it's not my business, as I'm sure you're about to tell me.'

'I just realised that if I keep my current job and get paid by you as well - to do nothing much which is truly incredible – then when I've paid off my dad's mortgage, I could afford to go back to university. I hadn't thought of that until just now, and it made me happy.'

He made no comment just smiled and pulled a folded paper out of his pocket. 'This is the contract. Check if it seems OK to you, and if anything needs changing I'll fix it. Or ask someone else to look it over.'

Alba stared at him. 'One page? A contract on a single sheet of paper?'

'A draft contract,' he said calmly and picked up his coffee cup. 'They make really good coffee here - I'm going to have another one. Would you like one too?'

She nodded and unfolded the paper, and when he returned with their coffees she shook her head at him. 'Have you got no sense of proportion? This is ridiculous.'

'Do you want more money? We can discuss it, no problem.'

'*More* money? My God, you *are* mad! It's far too much for mostly doing nothing at all. Way too much! Even if I give up my job in the warehouse and come to your office, so I could at least be useful every day, it's still more than I would have earned if I'd got that job I applied for. What on earth were you thinking?'

'Jesus, you're fierce when you get riled!' He sounded quite relaxed about it. 'I can't have you working in the office, you're my secret weapon. If I need you for a meeting at work, I'll tell everyone you're working for me privately on a new project or something and say you're just sitting in on some meetings. If you give me advance warning about even one person to avoid it would be worth it. I get approached by a lot of people who want me to go into some kind of venture with them, or they want money to start something, or they're trying to sell me something they've invented or developed, usually for big money. A couple of times I've had to use lawyers to get out of something that turned out to have a hidden fishhook.'

He saw her frown and added, 'I like to help people start new things and create new opportunities, so I sometimes finance things to help them get going, but it doesn't always turn out as it was supposed to. I'm not part of one of those angel investor groups. Maybe I should be, it might be safer – they probably have much better ways of evaluating start-up suggestions.'

'When you say they sometimes don't turn out the way you expected, is it because the idea they had didn't work, so you lost money?'

'No, it's not about the money - I don't mind losing the money I invest if things genuinely don't work out. But on a couple of occasions someone's used my name in a way they weren't supposed to, traded on my goodwill and implied I recommend their new business - or worse, that they were linked to my company, which happened just recently. Which was way outside the original agreement.'

Alba drank some coffee and thought about this, but before she could respond or object further he reverted to something they had talked about a couple of days ago. 'How do you know about the stock exchange?'

She looked hard at him. 'This might surprise you, but I did what most intelligent people do when they come across something they know nothing about, which I did last year when a friend of mine got one of those share trading apps. I Googled it, read four or five articles to get some different points of view, decided that even if I *could* afford to invest in shares I'd never to buy them via an app that relies on trading bots or any automated form of AI intervention, because it seems like a stupid idea. Enough information?'

'Yes, thanks, that tells me exactly what I expected.' He grinned and she knew he was waiting for her to ask what he had expected, but she drank some more coffee and waited.

'Anything you want to ask me?' he finally said.

'Yes, data crunching,' she said. 'You promised to tell me and then you didn't.'

'Ah yes, so I did. Well, this is what we did – we wrote a script that trawled though all the creditors in our accounting system and grabbed the ones that have been added or whose details have been changed over a given period of time, and then we cross-referenced those against real businesses with the same name, the genuine bank accounts of those businesses and the bank account numbers in our creditors ledger and compared them to what we had in the direct payment schedules that we send to the bank.'

His phone gave out a beep and he glanced at it and ignored it. 'Then we checked if the address and phone number entered as contact details really existed. We came across eight creditors that weren't legit, total fabrications and all entered into our system since Winterdale started with us three years ago. So, we took it one step further and double-checked things via the IT system audit trail, which showed who had initially entered those fake creditors and took it from there. The audit trail shows whose log-on was used, so it was very straight forward. Winterdale admitted everything in the second meeting we had with her, after we suggested she should bring a lawyer. When we showed them our findings, she owned up straight away.'

Alba was mesmerised by this revelation; to have been so right about that woman, to have the dread feeling confirmed as accurate for the first time, it felt like magic. On those previous occasions when it happened she had walked away and kept well clear of the person it had come from, and she had never known how real the threat had been. On one occasion she had wondered afterwards if it might have been her imagination, the person in question had seemed so unlikely, but she had been unable to stay, avoided him from then on and never found out if it was right.

'Great! The dread feeling *was* right,' she said now. 'Didn't the lawyer advise her to say nothing, like they do in the movies?'

Jake smiled grimly. 'Not when we showed them the evidence we had - it would have been useless. So, she'll be prosecuted for theft and fraud involving the fake creditors, and another thing we discovered as an extra bonus. She had recently created a ghost employee who didn't exist, which means the tax department is getting involved. Not to mention that the banks she used will prosecute her too for opening bank accounts under fake business identities. She'd put a lot of clever planning into it. So, you understand why I'm so grateful to you for talking to me about the dread feeling.'

For a few moments Alba silently gazed into the middle distance, re-living the moment when the dread feeling came over her in the interview room, recreating in her mind how it had felt.

'It was so strong. I knew I had to leave right away,' she said slowly and felt her toes curl in her shoes. 'We were right, she might have been dangerous for me to work with, maybe she could have implicated me in something. Just as you suggested, she might have been thinking of not only how she could fence me in, stop me discovering things, but actually do me harm personally? Or did I just get the dread feeling because of her general evilness?'

'I've no doubt you'll be a valuable asset, however it works. You might be the only one in the world who has this ability.'

He was serious, but she didn't want to be that serious, it felt uncomfortable to hear him say that, as if she were some kind of freak, not quite normal.

'Of course, I'm not. Korea's full of people who do this all the time. They get out of a line where they've been waiting for hours when they're nearly at the ticket office because they get the dread feeling and run all the way home. I'm half Korean, so I've got half the talent, if you can call it that.'

'And what are your plans for the rest of the day?' he asked, as if he sensed she felt unsettled and wanted to change the subject. 'Are you going back to work and then home to your dad?'

'First, I'm going back to work, and then I'm going home to get changed, and then I'm going out for dinner with an American guy I just met.'

He frowned. 'Who is this guy? Is he safe?'

'For God's sake, what *is* this? Are you turning into my father now? Of course, he's safe. He's not a thug or anything, he's a post-grad student. He's here for a year to study wetland ecology.'

'Well, don't go to his place after, please, not alone.'

'What on earth are you on about now?' She was outraged and amused at the same time. This was way outside what he had a right to ask. 'I might go to his place, or we might go to mine, or we might not go anywhere at all. This is ridiculous and it's *not* your business.'

'It *is* my business - I'm your boss and you're an asset.' She knew he was teasing now, just as certainly as she knew he had been totally serious when he told her not to go home with Ludo.

'And you're an ass. Don't keep calling me an asset! And you're not my boss.'

'Who's going to pay you?'

'OK, you'll soon be my boss, but you can't control what I do in my private life. It's an infringement of my human rights and my personal privacy. I can report you to some UN committee and you'll be lambasted in global media and have to go into hiding.'

'You know such wonderful words.'

He's laughing inside now, she thought, he likes being teased. Maybe people don't tease him because he's everybody's boss at work and powerful.

'I do, and I know some pretty bad ones too. Like, how about you stay the hell out of my private life, you big bully.'

She noticed the twitch at the corners of his mouth and choked back a laugh, then suddenly they were both laughing, nearly out of control. After a few moments he wiped his eyes and got serious. 'I apologise, I won't do it again. You're quite right, it's not my business what you do.'

'What is it you won't do again? Interfere in my life? Oh, *please* don't stop now, it gives me such lovely opportunities to hurl abuse at you – and maybe the occasional rock.'

But she smiled as she said it, because she was so enjoying this game they were playing that she couldn't stop herself, and she didn't want him to think she resented his comments. It's so weird, she thought, I've never in my life been so cheeky and outrageous with anyone, and I've only just met him, but I knew nearly right from the start that he'd know it was just playing. I could feel how much he enjoyed it, like a warm current coming my way.

'Do you mean that?'

'Oh, yes. I know you didn't mean it the way it sounded, and I can handle you.' She gave him a smug smile just to rub that last comment in and saw the look of disbelief.

'You think you can *handle* me? Really?'

'I've been doing it ever since we first met,' she said coolly. 'It's not that hard – you just hadn't noticed. It's a surreptitious form of stealth influence that I'm particularly good at.'

When they parted outside he turned at the last moment and looked hard at her, no hidden smile now. 'But will you please promise you won't be alone with this guy tonight unless someone else is in the house or flat or whatever?'

'Mr Boss-person, listen carefully now,' she said firmly and bit back the urge to laugh. 'In words of one syllable, or maybe two – I will *not* be alone with him, and I will *not* go to bed with him. Not now or at any time, *never-ever*! OK?'

'Thank you,' he said surprisingly and left her standing there looking after him with a frown. He'd be a great dad, she thought, and then she laughed and thought of how well he'd get on with her own father. But the idea of Jake as a dad made her feel funny, as if she was thinking something that verged on inappropriate. She shook herself as she walked away, and told herself she didn't really fancy him, she just liked him, and he thought she was young and cute, and he didn't mind being teased. He probably had a stack of glamorous women he took out, and maybe he had a favourite he went to bed with, she thought, someone who looked like a million dollars and knew how to please him, someone he regarded as an equal in age and whatever else mattered to him. She'd have to be careful not to reveal how attracted she was to him, how she felt that current when he touched her wrist – both times, like a fizzing streak of electricity running up her arm.

lba walked slowly from the bus stop towards the Korean restaurant that Ludo had suggested. She had nearly cancelled their date after his phone call, but she felt she must out of fairness give him a chance. Their phone conversation had given her a strong feeling that he wasn't her type at all, and arriving early or on time might make her seem keen, so she slowed her pace further, then stopped to look in a shop window to use up a bit of time.

Getting there ten or even fifteen minutes late was probably perfect, she thought, and stared unseeingly at the window display. There had been a hint of something a bit cringe-making about some of the things he said when he called, and she wasn't sure what was behind some of his comments. Maybe he regarded their date as a demonstration of his liberal attitudes to race or something else, or perhaps it was the fact that he deigned to date someone who worked in a warehouse. There had been a slight pause during their brief phone call when he asked where she worked, and she told him. And he had sounded so self-congratulatory when he told her how he had researched where to eat, as if she needed ethnically correct food. She tried to dispel the feeling of irritation and told herself not to be so judgmental. Perhaps he was just keen to avoid making her uncomfortable, but in that case he could have asked her where she would prefer to eat or what kind of food she liked, which would have signalled that he thought of them as equals.

When she arrived at the restaurant Ludo was patiently waiting outside and displayed no irritation about Alba being late. 'Hi,' he said cheerfully and held the door open. 'I wasn't sure which direction you'd be coming from, or I would have gone to meet you.'

'I was a bit late leaving,' said Alba untruthfully and hoped she sounded as if she didn't think this was anything she needed to apologise for. Let's see what he's made of, she thought when they were seated and had been given menus. The suspicion that she had made a mistake in accepting this date was being tempered now she was sitting opposite him. He was tall and blond and quite handsome, and she wondered if Linley's attitude to him at Blair and Carla's had somehow tainted her perceptions, so she had to be fair and give him a chance to prove he was not as bad as she had imagined.

They spoke little while they studied the menu,

and Alba wondered how familiar he was with Asian food of any kind, but the descriptions of the dishes were detailed, so it shouldn't be a problem.

'I'll have a small helping of the pork strips and kimchi, please,' said Alba to the waiter.

It was obvious that Ludo had researched the dishes online too and made himself familiar with what was in them, because he made his order with hardly a glance at the menu and said, 'What's your favourite dish? To make or to eat.'

Alba thought for a moment before she replied, tried to imagine why he had asked such a strange thing, but failed.

'I love cooking,' she said. 'I enjoy the whole process. I think my staple dinner party dish, which everyone apart from vegetarians loves, is Beef Stroganoff. I use my mum's recipe which seems to be a little different from most and it's delicious. Rich and flavoursome and given a long slow time in the oven the beef is so tender it melts in your mouth. I always serve it with Hasselback potatoes from a Swedish cookery book we have at home. And when it comes to eating ...' She paused and tried not to laugh at the expression on his face. 'I love Italian food, and pasta verde with grated parmesan is probably my favourite. So simple and so tasty. What about you?'

'I like American food,' said Ludo staunchly, as if admitting to liking something from another country might be close to disloyalty. But then he probably heard how parochial that made him sound and added, 'And I like Mexican food too, and I've learnt to really appreciate meat pies with a mashed potato topping, since I've been here - those individual ones. I hadn't had those before - and fish and chips, there's nothing better on a cold night. My roommate and I take turns going down the road to get fish and chips for dinner sometimes.'

There was a long silence after this statement, which Alba struggled to think of how to fill. Surely he was not this dull right through, there must be some hidden trait in his personality that she could winkle out, if she could only think of what to start with. Finally, she said, 'Are you a reader?' Asking him this had the benefit of an obvious follow-on question of what he liked to read most, and then they could compare favourite books and it would use up some conversational time.

For a moment he looked confused and then he smiled. 'Ah, you mean, do I read books? Yes, of course I do, loads of them and sometimes several at once. Like just now, I'm reading a very interesting book called Silt, Sand and Slurry which has some great theories about wetlands management, and at the same time I started a book this afternoon called Wetlands remediation in the tropics, which I got out of the university library and which I can see already is going give me some useful insights, things that would be applicable in Florida swamps for example.'

Alba tried to think of something they might have in common, something she could start a conversation about and hoped he wouldn't get the wrong idea if she asked about his family. So long as he didn't take it as some indication of deeper interest in him personally, she thought, but she would try to keep it within normal casual boundaries. They had to talk about something or sit in silence. By the time they had ordered dessert he was still describing his siblings, the church they attended and how much fun they had on family camping trips when he was a boy, and what a silly girl without any brains his younger brother was dating. But even with this seemingly endless supply of information and anecdotes, Alba felt increasingly desperate and thought she had never endured a meal that was so boring and so totally lacking in good conversation. At half past nine she was more than ready to go and made a pretence she knew was sneaky and below her, but necessary. She pretended to hear her phone vibrate and looked at it then at Ludo.

'I'm sorry, Ludo,' she said, 'I'm going to have to go to work very early tomorrow, two people can't come in, so I'll have to be there at six and have a very long day. I'd better get home and get some sleep – it's physical work and can be exhausting.'

And she was genuinely sorry. For him, who had so few clues about how to connect with a woman, and for herself for having to resort to such tricks.

But staying any longer felt impossible. They had nothing in common, he didn't read anything but books about his specialist field of study, he didn't like her jokes and throughout he had been condescending in a way that she now thought might not be based on race but on gender. He had been slightly dismissive when she voiced an opinion or questioned something he said. She thought of the Americans she had met on family holidays in the tropics, the friendship that had developed with the Bloom family from Montana they met in American Samoa, the fun she had on the trip to Fiji with a brother and sister from Maine and their parents, who had been happy to include her in all their activities and with whom she was still in touch. What rotten luck to end up on date with the only totally boring American she had ever met.

He accompanied her to the bus stop and waited until her bus arrived, and then he made a clumsy and disconcerting move. Just as the bus appeared in the distance, he suddenly grabbed her with one hand on her back and one on her backside and tried to kiss her. She turned her head away and swung out of his embrace, and he smiled. He's smiling! she thought, incredulous and speechless, he thinks I'm coy or something. As the bus stopped and the door opened he said, 'Next time let's go back to my place.'

Never have I met anyone so awkward, she thought and looked unseeingly out the window. And never before have I resorted to such underhand behaviour to get away from a man. He needs to find a nerd girl, a fellow student who can sit around and discuss wetland ecology over dinner, a girl he can manhandle into bed with no leadup and no consideration.

fter receiving Jake's next request for a meeting Alba asked for half a day off again and as usual Mark agreed.

'Of course,' he said, as if there was no need to ask. 'You can come in and help me on Saturday morning to make up for it. It's not as if we're dispatching fresh bread or something that will go off, is it? We'll finish it off on Saturday if there's any left to do. You're such a good worker – if you need time off just say.'

Once again Jake said he would meet her at the café at the local shopping centre, but this time she surprised him by paying for both of them. She whipped her ATM card out of her back pocket and swept if over the machine before he had time to react, and as she had expected he protested. The frown was back, and she thought, tough for you, but you need to learn you can't make everything happen just the way you want. You're so used to being the big boss that you can't switch off being the person who makes all the decisions.

'I was going to pay,' he said. 'There's no need for you to do it.'

'You paid in town and the last time we were here, but this is my home ground – and soon I'll be quite rich. Why do you want to come all the way out here, anyway? There are more places to go in the city. I don't get it - it's just silly!'

'Please don't take out your bad mood on me.'

'I'm not in a bad mood, but you were growling.'

'I never growl.'

'You *were* growling, and now you're scowling too. Growling and scowling like an angry pirate.'

'I don't scowl either.'

'You do so, you're doing it right now. It's a terrifying scowl, it's like being squashed by a very heavy weight and now I can't breathe properly.'

'What a terrible little liar you are! You don't look in the least bit scared.' She could tell he was holding back a smile.

She laughed. 'Of course, I'm not scared of you, don't be silly! Other people probably would be, but you wouldn't harm me or scare me away, I'm an asset.'

'So that still rankles, does it? How about we swap that word for another, so you can stop hurling it at me like one of your verbal rocks? Let's say you're special or precious - or irreplaceable, perhaps.'

That made her smile, and she stopped teasing

him. 'I think irreplaceable is going way too far, and I'm definitely not precious - let's say I'm special instead of an asset. Sorry I was rude, but I get the feeling you're so used to having your own way with everything that you don't understand when others might want different things. Going into town is a nice little break from every-day for me, so I just thought I'd push your world view around a bit now and again, just as a change for you - to brighten up your day.'

Now he smiled too, which made her happy. 'You're training me very well already, Alba - or handling me, I think you said. And I don't mind at all, just keep going. I'm beginning to enjoy it, you nasty little bully.'

'No, thanks. I'm finished now – for today, anyway.'

'And how was the date with the American?'

She narrowed her eyes at him. 'I *told* you I wasn't going to have sex with him! And I didn't. Do you want to know if he's a good kisser?'

'Is he?'

She laughed out loud. 'I have no idea. I didn't want to be kissed by him, so I didn't let him. And aside from all that, he's also very boring, the most boring man I've ever been out with. So, I just said goodbye very nicely and hopped on my bus.'

She saw the very moment when he remembered and cursed herself. She should never have mentioned the bus incident that first time they talked face to face. It was something she had never told anyone, and she hoped she would be able to deflect him and change the subject. She'd known at the time that if he ever asked about it again she must divert him, because it had been so frightening that she couldn't bear to talk about it. She still had heart-stopping nightmares about it and what might have happened to her if she hadn't got away.

'What's the matter? Are you OK?' He looked concerned, and she realised her feelings were visible on her face. I hope he doesn't think he's upset me, she thought, I'll have to explain a little, so he knows it's not his fault, that it just made me feel upset even thinking about that man.

'You were just about to ask about the dread thing with the man on the bus, weren't you? Don't look so surprised, I could see the moment you remembered that I refused to answer when you asked about it before. It was horrible, it scared me so much I never take the late-night bus now in case I see him again. So, no more going into the city for things that finish late.'

She stopped talking and tried to dispel the feeling of remembered threat, how she ran through the dark streets with her heart pounding so hard it felt as if it would erupt out of her chest, and how she didn't dare turn to look behind her in case she tripped and fell.

Jake was watching her closely, and she could see how worried he was now, more so every moment. Maybe she should tell him the whole thing, make someone else understand how terrifying it had been and possibly be able to consign the memory to some remote storage place in her mind. She took a deep breath.

'This is how it was. I was on the bus back from town very late. I'd had a late lecture and then three of us went to a movie, and after the movie we went to have pizza,' she said quietly. 'It was winter and cold, and I got frozen waiting for the bus. I didn't have a jacket, well that's not part of the story, I just remember standing there wishing the bus would come soon. Most people got off the bus before we got to Onehunga, and then two stops before mine a man got on. The moment the bus started up, the very second he turned and looked down the length of the bus I got the dread feeling very strongly. I nearly ran up to the front to ask the driver to let me out, but then I thought, what if he gets out too? I didn't know what to do, it was the most evil-feeling thing I'd ever experienced, I was terrified.'

She was speaking faster and faster and stopped for a moment, told herself to breathe properly, to slow down. She cleared her throat and continued. 'So, I made a panicky plan, and at the next stop, one before mine, a woman got on and I went and stood by the door in the middle of the bus, as if I was about to get off, and the driver saw me in his mirror and opened the doors, but I didn't get out. I stayed where I was. I could see that man watching me, ready to get up and get off too, it was as clear as daylight, his eyes were fixed on me the whole time and he had that tensed muscle look, ready leap to his feet – and the dread feeling was nearly choking me.'

She ran out of breath again and stopped, and Jake put his hand on top of hers, and that firm, warm hand steadied her, and she thought 'safety, it feels like safety'. She took another deep breath and continued. 'But at the very last second, when the door made that funny little sound it makes when the closing mechanism turns on, I just leapt out, crazy fast and half tripped – I nearly fell flat on my face. So, I managed to get out and he didn't. And then I ran.'

'Christ!' said Jake and his hand tightened on hers. 'You were scared out of your mind. I can see it on your face now.'

'I hadn't realised how hard it would be to tell someone. I haven't told anyone before and it makes me feel terrified just talking about it – it's weird, it's like it's happening right now,' she said, and she could hear her own voice starting to crack again. She pulled herself together, took a deep breath and continued. 'Anyway, I just ran and ran as fast as I could, and I went round random corners and down a long alleyway between some houses, just hoping to get far away, way over to one side from the street where I'd jumped out, so he wouldn't find me. I mean in case he'd managed to get the driver to stop and let him off, too, but I didn't dare turn around to see if he was behind me in case I tripped.'

She was speaking very fast again, she just wanted to get it over with. 'I dream about it sometimes, that he catches up with me and what he would do to me … and then I wake up in a panic and my heart is beating so fast it scares me.'

She mentally shook herself to try and dispel the feeling of oppressive fear. Talking about it had infused her with a nearly physical sensation of danger, like a low-level version of how she had felt at the time. She had hoped that maybe if she told somebody else it would lessen the power the incident had to disturb her, but it seemed to have had the opposite effect. Jake lifted his hand off hers and got up. 'Come on, we'll go and sit at the table outside in the sun.'

She followed him outside, still tense but also relieved that she had finally told someone about it. Ever since it happened she had kept it to herself, concerned about how Steve or Linley, who were the only ones she might tell, would react, how worried they would be.

Once they were outside, instead of sitting down at the little pavement table, Jake took a step to the side and said, 'Come here.'

He pulled her in, put his arms around her and held her tight against his chest. 'It's OK now, I've got you.' He spoke quietly into the top of her head, and she felt his warm breath through her hair. 'I understand how scared you were, but you're safe now. Just breathe deeply and you'll feel better soon.'

She felt his hand move to her shoulder as if he were making sure she was securely anchored against him, and she sighed. Gradually her heartbeat slowed, she felt she could breathe properly again and relaxed against him. They stood there for what seemed like a long time, but it was probably only a minute or two, close together, not speaking or moving, then she took a step back and he let her go.

She felt as if she had emerged from a cocoon where she had been insulated from the world, safe and protected. She looked up at him and said so quietly it was nearly a whisper, 'Thank you!'

Jake smiled and motioned toward the little table. 'Let's sit down and plan our approach for that business meeting.'

Lightening the mood seemed important to Alba and she said, 'Could we have another coffee while we talk? I'll let you pay this time.'

With coffee and biscuits in front of them, he picked up where he'd left off. 'It's a preliminary meeting with some people who want to set up two companies. One owned by us jointly which in turn will own the second company - for joint use by the group, a shell company,' he said and now the pirate frown was back, but she decided not to mention it. 'To be used when one in the group wants to acquire an asset, maybe buy a business that operates in opposition in order to close it down, like asset stripping and market control in one move. A shell company to funnel funds through in order to enable take-overs of small businesses more or less on the quiet, without the names of large companies and well-known investors being so obvious. I'm sure you can see why they want this?'

'Of course – if the little companies knew who was trying to buy them up, if they knew it was companies or people with a lot of money, they'd ramp up the price and negotiate harder. Two companies, like in layers, to make it less obvious who's behind it.'

'Smart girl!' said Jake. 'You never disappoint me. This kind of venture isn't something I want to be part of, but they've approached me, and I've agreed to this meeting with them because I want to find out why they want me to come in with them. Is it because I have the financial ability to do things like buy up competing companies, maybe help fund the others to do so? Or are they after something else?' He thought for a moment. 'I have a strong suspicion I'm being used, which is why I need you there. In this meeting I don't want you to be a so-called project leader, not in front of these guys. I'd like to introduce you as a schoolgirl on a work experience assignment, if you don't mind dressing just like you did the first time we met?'

'Why?'

'To disarm them, I suppose you could say. Make them think you're a cute, little harmless girl who won't understand half of what they say. One of them is a good friend of mine, Adam, and he's bringing a guy he knows. What I really want to find out is why they want me involved, and I think the second guy, Adam's friend, is the driving force here.

Very likely he's involved Adam as a means of getting to me. But why me? I really want to find out what the subtext is, something I can't put my finger on. Once I figure it out, I can warn Adam away from this because it's just the sort of thing that might backfire, and though he's OK financially, he can't afford to lose big sums of money on investments gone wrong. Oh, and an older man called Gregory will be there, too, but he's OK. I'm not worried about him.'

She tried to imagine the situation she would be in, four men and only one of them known to her. Three who would take whatever Jake told them about her as true, but what might they ask her? Would they ask personal questions?

'If I'm doing a school project,' she said having thought through various alternatives, 'what would you like it be? They might ask me. Are they likely to ask me personal questions, do you think?'

'I doubt they'll ask you anything personal. I'll introduce you and tell them you're doing this as an extension of the normal kind of work experience if you like. You can tell them what you think the title of the project should be if they ask. Otherwise just sit quietly like a good schoolgirl would. Something relating to business or accounting or social studies – you went to school more recently than I did, you can decide.'

She thought for a few seconds. 'Let's say the title of the project is "different formats of business meetings and what benefits might accrue from them." And I can say it's an observational study using de-linked evaluation tools – that will baffle them.'

'Jesus, how did you come up with that so fast? Let's use that exactly as you said it, just the kind of business garbage they teach people these days. And what are de-linked evaluation tools?'

'I've no idea, I just made it up, so I can confuse them with jargon.'

That made him laugh. 'OK, very clever – again. So, you come into town on Wednesday the week after next, the fourteenth. We'll meet somewhere around the corner from the hotel where I'm meeting these guys, just in case they are early - so we're seen to arrive together. But we'll hopefully be there before them, so we can organise how we sit. I imagine both of us facing them might be important. I'll text the time and the place.' He gave her a wry smile. 'They turned down the offer to meet in my office, which made me even more suspicious, and said they'd book a space where we could be private. Remember to dress like a kid and could you do your hair in a topknot like the first time I met you? They'll be totally taken in, just like I was.'

Just as they parted to walk away in opposite directions he said, 'I like you in that T-shirt – you look very pretty in blue.'

She stood still and watched him walk away and thought how out of character that comment was compared to anything else he had ever said to her. She liked that he noticed that the colour suited her, but then she shook herself and started jogging back to the warehouse and told herself to stop being an idiot. A stray comment and the fact that he had comforted her after the bus story, those things meant nothing more than kindness. A man like him wouldn't be interested in her, not in any real way, he was just being nice. She tried not to think about how she had felt when he held her tight against his chest, the way his hand had moved to her shoulder, and how safe she had felt, as if nothing could harm her or scare her. Don't dwell on it, she told herself and started running, don't be an idiot about this, it meant nothing to him, so don't start imagining things.

ow that she had met with Jake again and accepted the job, Alba couldn't wait to tell her father about both the contract and the prospect ahead of her. On Sunday mornings they usually had porridge or toast, sometimes both, instead of just cereal like on weekdays. While Steve made porridge Alba set the table and looked after the toaster, waiting patiently and trying to keep the news about the job inside her and not let it just burst out. When they finally sat down with bowls of porridge with brown sugar sprinkled over it the way they both liked it, she said, 'I've got something really exciting to tell you, dad! You remember that job I applied for in town a couple months ago, and then I walked out halfway through the second interview? Well, I've got a job there anyway!'

'Really?' said Steve surprised and pleased. 'Same job? What about the dread feeling?'

'No, not even in the office. I'll be hired privately

by the CEO.' She waited for what she knew would come, enjoying in advance how suspicious he would be before she explained, but his expression of alarm made her instantly feel guilty.

He sat up straighter and sent a hard look across the table. 'What? How did this happen? It doesn't sound right to me – and how do you know you can trust this guy? Is he really the CEO? Honestly, Alba, you can't have thought this through, it sounds crazy.'

'Sorry, dad! That was evil, but I just wanted to see what you'd say. I really have been offered a job and he isn't just the CEO. He started that huge tech company and holds more shares than anyone else, and it's all above board.'

'Ah,' he said, relieved. 'You're so like your mother, not just in looks but that naughty, impulsive side I sometimes worry about. One day you'll go too far and get into trouble, you know. So, tell me what this job really is and when you start.'

Alba spooned in another mouthful of porridge and tried to decide how to present this, because she hadn't counted on quite such a strong reaction. And then she got it, put the spoon down and said, 'No, dad – I'm not going to answer questions. I'm going to tell you a long, long story with lots of ins and outs and details. And you'll have to sit really still and listen to the whole thing, OK?'

'Miss Bossy has moved back in, has she?' said Steve. 'If it's a long story we might want to make another coffee first, I think.'

They finished their porridge, made another cup of coffee to have with the toast, and Alba started telling the story. Now she had worked it through in her mind and knew it had to be told in chronological order, from the first call from Jake, right down the track of texts, calls and meetings, including all Jake had said and what she had said. It was important that Steve could understand how she had come to trust Jake and knew with deep conviction that he was upfront and honest. And in addition, she realised just as she was starting, she must somehow fit in her rationale for whatever she had said and done as she went along, or he would interrupt a hundred times – she knew well how protective he was and how the slightest hint of anything suspect would alarm him.

Putting her elbows on the table and leaning forward, intent on making him listen calmly, she had only got to the part about the first meeting in a café after Jake told her about the fraud at MoreIT and how she told Jake to go get a whore somewhere else, before her father jerked on his chair, and she knew he was going to interrupt.

'Hang on, dad! Just wait till you hear the rest.'

Reluctantly he sat back and said nothing, and she continued, but a moment later he reacted strongly again. 'He grabbed hold of your wrist? Is this man safe to be with? Honestly, Alba, maybe he's tricked you and he's just pretending to be the CEO. He might be some kind of predator.'

If this was going to work she must tell him a bit

more about Jake, not in the order she had planned, but more from the angle of how she decided that she could trust him. She would give her father a picture of how she had treated Jake with pretend admonitions and rebuke, abused him and laughed at him, and how Jake's hidden smile had finally emerged into outright laughter from where she had felt it lurking the moment she met him.

'So, you see I was right from the start, don't you? He was so serious and so much the super successful businessman, and he's so used to having his own way and people just doing whatever he tells them, but I got him to let go. I knew nearly from the start that he had another persona inside that very firm, serious exterior. I could see that little muscle tightening at the corner of his mouth when he was trying not to laugh when I mock-abused him.'

Her father gave her a thoughtful look that she couldn't quite interpret and sat back again, seeming to have accepted that Jake was above board. When she told him how she told Jake he was like the elephant's child, Steve laughed out loud, and she nearly confessed that she called him a big bully, too, but lightning fast she realised that it would involve explaining the rest of that conversation, so she said nothing about it. Neither did she mention that strange little exchange when he made her promise never to change. Too personal, she thought and drank some of her nearly cold coffee, too open to misunderstandings. Not that she understood it herself, but she knew there was some tenuous significance there, some warning or promise that she preferred not to dwell on.

Now that Alba realised that many things from that point onwards might be alarming or misunderstood by her father she would be careful what she revealed. No way would she tell him how Jake had asked her to not go somewhere on her own with Ludo, or what she had said in reply. Neither could she relate the story about the man on the bus, and how Jake held her in that tight hug and how it had made her feel, when she was so upset after telling him. She made a snap decision and jumped straight to the contract, how she had protested and how Jake thought she wanted more money.

'I couldn't believe it,' she said seriously. 'He thought I wasn't satisfied with being offered a full-time salary for doing practically nothing! I told him he was mad, but he said, no, he was happy to use me as a truth filter, that's what he called it, and he said it was worth it even if it worked only once, or not at all. Apparently he gets approached by people who have all kinds of schemes in mind, things they think he might invest in or will lend his name to, and he wants me to sit in on some meetings and see if I get the dread feeling about any of them.'

'Holy hell!' said Steve. 'What a weird thing, I've never heard of anything like it. It sounds like a TV drama or something, nearly like science fiction.'

'I know, it's kind of crazy, but it's exciting too. And if he's prepared to try it, I'm not saying no to an extra income. Let's face it, none of us know how that dread thing works, do we? It could be that it only works when it's all about me, someone posing some kind of threat to me, or maybe just thinking of doing me harm. Or it could be when I'm present and someone is posing a threat to someone else in the room, thinking of doing nasty things or whatever. So, Jake's happy to try it as an experiment, and meanwhile I'll have two incomes, and we'll pay off that mortgage much faster. Isn't it great? All I need to do is ask at work if I can have a day off now and then and make it up in the weekends.'

'Do you really want to keep the warehouse job?'

'Oh, yes, of course I will. What else am I going to do with my time? Take up knitting?'

They tidied up the kitchen and Alba went to start the washing machine while her father mowed the lawn, and nothing more was said about it until after dinner, when they were watching a film on Netflix.

'Dad, can you pause that for second? I've just thought of something I've read about. You know how people can ask for a mortgage holiday if they have financial troubles, and they just pay the interest on their mortgage for a while and leave out the portion that repays the capital?'

Steve looked confused. 'Yeah, but we don't need a mortgage holiday – the opposite, in fact.'

'Yes, I know,' she grinned. 'As I've said to Jake once or twice, I'm not stupid! But maybe you can ask the bank to shorten the term of the mortgage and pay off more each week or month, so it gets paid off sooner? If they can let people have mortgage holidays, you'd think they could do the opposite too, wouldn't you?'

A text from Jake about the meeting arrived late that evening when Alba was reading in bed.

'I forgot to give you a copy of the signed contract. Remind me on 14th. And invent a fake name for me to introduce you by, nothing like your real name.'

'Tell them I'm Maria Kim. People think all Koreans are called Kim or Ko.'

'Aren't they all called Park?'

'Some are called Asher.'

10

On Monday Alba made sure she kept an eye on Mark, her boss, so she could coordinate her lunch break with his. The whole team worked independently and usually took their breaks when it suited them, and **she** wanted to talk to Mark undisturbed. The huge warehouse was very hot on sunny days, and she had left her water bottle in the lunchroom, but she made herself wait until she spotted Mark heading toward the loading bay just after one. She abandoned the trolley of half-filled boxes and set out down the long central aisle after him. Before skirting around the electric forklift, she checked carefully that it was empty. The near incident earlier in the year when she had cut behind it just as it started reversing, at the very moment the beeps started, had given her a fright and taught her to be very cautious. Shane, who had been driving it at the time, had been white-faced with fright.

'I could have killed you!' he had shouted. 'You were so damn close and you're short – I never saw you in the mirrors. Don't you ever do that again!'

She had waited for Mark to have lunch, because she knew that if the other three packers were having lunch right then they would be outside in the sun where they kept some plastic chairs in the sheltered corner next to the dumpster where they could smoke. She wanted to talk to Mark without being overheard by the others asking for a favour again and then seen as someone who got special treatment, and this time it would take longer to explain.

In the lunchroom she took her wrapped sandwich and water bottle out of the little fridge and sat down opposite Mark. 'Why don't you ever sit outside with the other guys? On sunny days it's always just you and me in here, and sometimes even when it rains – they sit on the edge of the loading dock so they can smoke.'

'That's why I wouldn't go near them, they all smoke.' Mark grinned. 'And why don't you sit out there in the sun yourself?'

Alba shrugged. 'I don't ever try to get a tan, I'm very careful. I want nice, smooth skin when I'm old. Too much ultraviolet turns you into a dried prune. It's a Korean thing my mum taught me.'

She bit into her sandwich and chewed, drank some water from her bottle and said, 'Look, this isn't going to sound great and if it doesn't work for you, just say. I've been offered a chance to sit in on some negotiations – financial stuff – via someone I know. It will only happen now and then, but when it does I'll probably need the whole day off. I'd always make up the time the following weekend, but I can't tell you exactly when it might happne, I might not get a lot of notice.'

Mark seemed unfazed by this vague outline and waved his own sandwich towards the door. 'Look at that lot – only one of them ever comes in to give me a hand in the weekend if we're behind. Sandy and you are the only two who do, so I don't mind at all. You should take every opportunity you can to learn things, Alba, and then go back to your studies. You're a clever girl.'

That evening she told Steve about the conversation with Mark, and he seemed unsurprised. 'I never expected him to say anything else. He knows you work hard and do extra when it's needed, and he wouldn't want to lose you. Did I tell you about next Saturday?'

'No, what's happening on Saturday?' she asked, but she knew it was most likely one of two things: either a vintage car meet in a park somewhere or the brass band having been booked to play at some event.

'The band's been hired to play at a big vintage car display at Henderson Park,' he said, and Alba nearly laughed at how her guess had proved doubly right.

'Perfect!' she said. 'You'll be able to march around and look at the cars at the same time.'

'No marching,' said Steve. 'They don't need the whole lot of us – it's not as if we're going to do formation marching or anything. We'll just stand around playing on and off for a couple of hours in the middle of the day. They want the big band jazz sound - you know, like the bands from the thirties and forties, same era as the cars, I suppose. I'll probably be gone the whole day – lots to look at after we play.'

'Oh, great!' said Alba. 'I was thinking of doing one of longer treks in the Hunua ranges, probably that steep one over to the side, where you get the views, and where I'll not be with all the families and kids. I'll take the opportunity while we still have mum's car.'

Steve bent to peer into the oven. 'Do you think this is roasted enough now? It's ages since you put it in.'

'Dad, it's not ages!' She looked her phone. 'It's only been thirty-five minutes. I'll tell you when it's ready if you want to go out and do something in the garden while it's still light enough.'

When they sat down to their roast chicken dinner Steve reached for the tomato salad and surprised her by saying, 'Are you sure you don't want to keep the car now that you'll have two incomes? It's a good car.'

'Oh no, I don't need a car. Let's sell it and get rid of that mortgage as soon as we can – in case this truth-filter job doesn't last. If we put all the money we can lay our hands on towards paying off the mortgage, we'll be rid of it in no time.'

She could see he wasn't convinced, but the car was an unnecessary luxury, and if she went out at night she could borrow Steve's utility truck. Changing the subject seemed like a good idea now before they ended up discussing the car right through dinner.

'Could you pass the tomato salad, please? Do you like the way I did the dressing with balsamic vinegar?'

A text message from Linley arrived just as Alba was getting into bed: *Do you want to meet for lunch tomorrow and some shopping?*

Alba replied: *No thanks. Do you want to come for a 5-hour trek in the Hunuas instead?*

She kept the phone in her hand and waited for the reply from Linley, which she could guess nearly word for word, and a minute later she laughed at Linley's response: *Can't think of anything I'd less like to do! But thanks for asking.*

On Saturday morning Alba did what she had done many times before when she was about to set out on one of her lonely treks in the Hunua regional park. She loved solitary walks and hardly ever asked anyone to come with her. The feeling of not having to talk and not feeling obliged to wait for someone who walked more slowly, the smell of the native bush and the bird song was a recharge activity she had treasured ever since a boyfriend had taken her there when she was a teenager.

Straight after breakfast she packed her little daypack while her father sat on a kitchen stool polishing his black shoes, already dressed in his band uniform trousers. For Alba it was a routine that needed no thought: a nut-and-raisin bar and a drink bottle of water, her phone and a peanut butter sandwich wrapped in cling film. She stuffed her waterproof jacket and a beanie in on top and closed the bag.

'Right!' she said. 'I'll be off now, so I'll see you some time near the end of the day. There's one of those quick-heat pizzas in the freezer, so if you're home before me you can get it out to thaw. They always taste better if you bake them thawed.'

The further Alba got from the shorter and easier walks, the happier she was because up here it was quiet. There were no human voices and no shrieks from children shouting to each other as they ran ahead of their parents, nothing like the easier loop track she had started out on. The only sound was bird song and the occasional strong wind gust ruffling the tree canopy, and once the raucous shriek of a falcon flying overhead, though she couldn't see it. A light drizzle of rain made her consider getting her jacket out of her pack, but looking up she could see blue sky to the west and decided it wasn't worth it.

A couple of hours later when she stopped to have a drink, the rain started falling in earnest, so she put the jacket and the beanie on and continued with the pack in her hand. She would go to the highest point of the track, which she knew was no more than a few hundred meters ahead of her, look at the wider cloud cover and decide if she should turn around or continue. Up on the high ridge, where the ground sloped steeply away on both sides the track took up practically the entire width of the crest with views in all directions. She could see heavy rain coming in from the east and decided to turn around before it reached her. She pulled the zip up to her chin and turned, and at that very moment the edge of the track gave way right in front of her. A cascade of dirt and rocks slid down the steeper side, and she took a quick step backwards just in time before another slice of the ridge fell away. Retreating another couple of steps, she studied what was left of the narrow strip of land where the track had suddenly been reduced to a much narrower band of solid looking ground.

Was it safe or would more give way if she stepped on it? She leaned over to one side to check there was no gap under what remained of the track, no illusion of solid ground with an empty space under it, but it looked OK, and she considered her options. She could continue further into the hills and possibly get back to her starting point in another three hours or she could get across the crumbling part of the path, which would probably only require five or six fast steps and return the way she had come in half the time, an easier and faster walk, and most of it under the tree canopy, so less exposed to the rain that was clearly coming in fast.

Halfway across the narrow band of track she lost her footing as the ground gave way under her. She fell in a shower of dirt and stones, closed her eyes and flung one arm across her face as she tumbled down the nearly vertical slope with rocks and mud coming down all around her. Up and down ceased to have a meaning, a bigger rock hit her shoulder hard, and then suddenly she was caught on something that rocked violently up and down. Her eyes flew open, and she instinctively grabbed hold and held on for dear life. A branch! She was on a long, heavy pine tree branch that still rocked with her weight on it. She looked down at where the cascade of mud and rocks had now disappeared down the slope. The tree she was caught in had its roots way down the steep side of the ravine, possibly ten metres further down than the branch that had caught her. Her heart was pounding, and she stifled a sob of fear as she held on tight and tried to think of what to do. The branch was still rocking, but more gently now and her breathing slowed. The grip of her hands couldn't possibly be enough to balance her, something held her in place. She let go with one hand and nearly rolled to one side, quickly put the hand back and held on tight, but in that little movement she had felt something, and she risked slowly turning her head to look back over her shoulder. The rain fell on into her eyes when she turned her head, but she saw enough. She was more than halfway in along the branch with a side shoot like a thick arm covered with long pine needles sticking up between her legs. A tiny wriggle and she felt the hard core of it against her inner thighs. She clamped her legs together, comforted by the idea that she wasn't only relying on the grip of her hands.

To be safe she must get closer to the trunk, where the branch would rock less and there was less risk of falling. She must somehow inch forward, but it meant moving away from the support between her legs. Resting her head on her outstretched arms she tried to estimate the risk involved in moving. The only way she could move further in towards the tree trunk would be by wriggling along the branch on her stomach, pulling with her hands and trying to grip with her legs, and somehow working her way past side-shoots all along its length.

It took her a long time to feel brave enough to risk the first move. The thought of falling to the ground from this height made her stomach clench with fear and she delayed making a move, but the feeling of lying on something that moved in the wind was unsettling. She would feel much safer leaning against the trunk.

She clamped both hands tight onto the branch in front of her and tried to haul herself along, but all it achieved was to set the branch rocking violently again. The thought of the branch cracking away from the tree and sending her headlong down the slope nearly made her change her mind. It took a long time to work out how to slowly and labouriously manoeuvre herself into a position where she could simultaneously lift her body a fraction by clamping her knees against the branch and then slowly inch forward, reaching with her hands to a new point to grip. Her hands were cold and wet, and now that she had left the side-shoot that had caught between her legs, she felt insecure, terrified of making a wrong move. Getting past the side-shoots was less scary than it had seemed, each shoot provided more stability and something to grip, though lifting her legs over them made the branch rock violently.

While the rain intensified and it seemed as dark as dusk already, she worked her way closer to the trunk, inch by inch and talking aloud to herself, telling herself she was strong, she could do it. But the struggle didn't end when she finally reached the trunk because first she had to sit up and move even closer, and then she must somehow turn herself around, an operation that made her nearly despair. Could she do it? Was it taking too great a risk? She could sit facing the trunk and wait for help, but she nearly instantly rejected the idea. She needed to be able to look up towards the ridge. The thought that someone might stand up there and miss seeing her if she couldn't attract their attention spurred her into reluctant action. Time ceased to have meaning, she twisted and pulled, hooked her legs around the branch and managed to sit up, then continued to slowly pull herself forward until she was sitting upright resting her forehead against the rough bark of the tree. Then another long interval of doubt and fear before she began the process of turning around, straddle the branch and lean back against the trunk. In the end the only thing that made it possible was a small branch above her and to the left that she could just reach to steady herself.

When Alba finally took stock, the rain was still falling steadily, the sky was covered in dark clouds and the temperature was dropping. With the immediate danger over, she tried to make a plan, but nothing much came to mind, as she stared down at her hands covered in scratches and sap, sticky and dark with dirt. Absentmindedly she rubbed her hands against her thighs, but nothing appeared to come off and her jeans were nearly as filthy as her hands anyway.

'OK,' she said aloud to herself. 'I'm wet and cold, my pack is way down there in that damn ravine, and I have no water, no phone and no food.'

What could she do? Nothing much, she decided after a moment. There was no way of signalling where she was, she had seen nobody for at least the last hour on the track, so nobody was likely to come past. Help would be slow coming. But she was cold now that she had stopped struggling to get to her safe perch. The beanie was lost, but she unzipped her jacket, blessed the chance that had made her put on a hooded sweatshirt that morning, dragged the hood out from under the jacket and pulled it over her wet hair.

'That's better,' she told herself, slightly cheered by hearing a voice, even if it was only her own. 'Pull the hood up, tighten the drawstring – good thing I didn't pull it out when I bought this top like I usually do with those irritating dangly bits. That's much better! And now I'll zip myself up again, right up and pull the jacket hood up over the top. Perfect! Nice and warm and waterproof all over expect for my legs.' She pulled the hood's adjustable string tighter to seal it around her face and felt she had achieved something, however little.

Time passed slowly and she leaned back against the trunk of the tree, exhausted now. She had no idea what the time was or how long it would be before her father missed her. What will he do? she wondered and tried to imagine how he would start worrying when it got dark, and whom he might ask for help. Will he drive out here when it's late and I don't answer my phone. I wonder if my phone is connecting to the network, so they can get my position via GPS. I wonder how soon they'll send out a search party if he tells the police I'm missing. He'll see my car if he comes out here, it will be the only one left in the parking area, but the tracks go for miles and miles, and nobody knows which one I'm on.

Without warning she started to cry, quietly sobbing into her filthy hands without understanding why she was crying. After a while her tears stopped as suddenly as they had started, and when she looked up she realised it was dark, it was early evening. She could see nothing, not even the outline of the ridge high above her and felt very insecure, sitting high up in a tree with no visual reference points.

She licked rain off her jacket sleeves to quench her thirst and thought longingly of her peanut butter sandwich and the nearly full water bottle in her pack. Next time she would wear the pack all the time and she would keep her phone in her inside jacket pocket. There would be no more assumptions that a real emergency wouldn't occur on an innocent day-walk; everything would be thought out in advance, and she would be prepared for every potential disaster.

After a while the need to pee became urgent but she ignored it for a while, hoping for magic to present an acceptable solution. After repeatedly telling herself that she was being ridiculous and that peeing in her clothes in an emergency such as this was nothing to worry about, she finally decided she had to do it, but letting go was another matter. She tried to make it happen, but inhibitions from childhood about wetting your pants made it hard.

She wriggled a bit on her branch and finally managed, and for a few minutes the warm wet feeling was quite nice, but the night air soon turned her wet jeans into cold, clammy misery.

Through that night Alba snoozed in short bursts interspersed with jerking awake from dreams about falling. During one short nap she dreamed that Jake was holding her safe, clasped against his chest, and she could feel his hand on her shoulder anchoring her, but when she woke up properly she was still alone in the dark and nobody was holding her. The wind rushed through the treetops she couldn't see, there was no sound apart from nature's night noises and the occasional, sudden hard shower of rain hitting the branches around her. When dawn finally broke the rain had stopped and the sky was clearing.

11

Not long after dawn Alba heard a man's voice repeatedly calling her name from far away and she sat up straight and listened until he was a bit closer and then closer still and yelled back as loudly as she could: 'I'm down here, in the ravine! In a tree – look down where the track is broken.'

After repeating this a couple of times, the voice came from right above her and through the branches she saw a man in a fluorescent jacket standing on the edge of the track, close to the large scallop of missing ground and looking straight down at her.

'Shit, girl – that's bad!' he said in a loud voice. 'Are you OK? How the hell did you end up there?'

'The slip took me with it,' she called back. 'The track crumbled under my feet. I fell and got caught on this branch, and then I worked my way in towards the trunk. Can you get me down?'

'No way, far too steep and dangerous! We'll have to get the helicopter in to lift you out. Your dad's down in the car park. I'll call down on the radio to the others down there and let him know I've found you.'

She heard parts of the conversation he had with her father because this was a man who had never learnt to moderate his voice. 'Yep, she seems unharmed. Yeah, way up high in a tree on a vertical slope on that east-west ridge. The track fell away and took her with it. I've called the chopper and given them the GPS coordinates. Oh no, tell him not to do that! We'll have her down in the car park in an hour or so, long before he could get here and there's nothing he could do here anyway.'

'They say your dad wants me to take a photo of you,' he called down to her, amused by the idea. 'Not much point, you're well hidden in that tree, but I'll try.'

Forty minutes later, the helicopter hovered above her and a man was winched down in a storm of swirling air and wildly tossing branches, but the operation took a lot longer than she had thought it would, because he couldn't get close to the trunk of the tree.

'Hold on tight so you don't blow off that branch,' he shouted from where he dangled quite a distance to the side of her tree, and Alba could only just hear him over the noise of the helicopter. 'Just wait - I'll try to swing in.'

He made it on the sixth attempt, when the

momentum of the swing got him within reach and ignoring her hand held out to grab his, he got hold of the branch directly above her.

'Now listen,' he shouted. 'This is going to be a bit scary, but you've got to do exactly what I tell you. First grab this harness that I'm going to toss to you – it's attached to me so you can't lose it. I'll tell you how to strap it on while you're sitting down, then I'll righten the strap and you get up and stand on your branch, OK? Then I'll pull it tighter and let go of my branch, and you'll have to step off your branch at the same time and we'll both swing like mad and get winched up. I'll count to three once you're standing up.'

After a few terrifying moments, first stepping out into empty space and then feeling the harness jerk her up, Alba found herself dangling a couple of metres below her rescuer, tethered to him by a strap that seemed dangerously thin. And there was the helicopter, straight above her and the downdraft washed over her and forced her to close her eyes. A minute later they were both inside and unhooked, and the door was shut.

'Well done!' shouted the man who had pulled them in and passed her a water bottle. 'Bet you're thirsty! My God, you're filthy, you poor thing.'

'It won't come off,' she shouted back when he held out a packet of wet wipes and drank thirstily before she continued. 'I'm covered in sap and stuff. It doesn't matter.'

She unzipped her jacket and pulled the

sweatshirt hood from her head and suddenly the world seemed to be back to the way it should be, ordinary and unthreatening. Not that she had ever been in a helicopter before, but they were part of the regular world, a long way from her frightening dreams in the night. A few minutes later they landed in the parking lot, she was helped out and was nearly swept off her feet by the blast from the rotor when her rescuer let go of her arm. Her father was coming towards her at a half run and Alba smiled to show him that she was all right as she ran to meet him.

'Don't hug me, dad! I'm covered in pine sap,' she said when they had moved out of the blast of air. 'It's very sticky stuff and impossible to rub off. God, I can't wait to get home!'

It was only then she saw Jake standing to one side watching the reunion scene. When he saw that she had noticed him he came forward, grabbed her shoulders in a hard grip and studied her face. 'Are you OK? You're not hurt?'

'No, I'm fine, I'm just tired. I didn't get much sleep up in that tree. What are *you* doing here?'

It was strange to see him in this setting and that brief dream from the night made it stranger still, like some kind of link had been established between them without her being aware of it happening. He was dressed for tramping and her heart made a little jump when she realised he had been ready to go and look for her. Amazed she stared up into his face and then she smiled the smile her mother used to call her naughty smile. 'Didn't want to lose an asset, did you, Mr Boss-person?'

'That's my girl!' he said quietly and let go of her shoulders.

Steve drove Alba back in her car, with her sitting in the passenger seat on her inside-out jacket to avoid getting sap on the upholstery, while Jake drover her father's utility truck behind them.

'How on earth did he know about this?' she said after trying in vain to sort it out in her mind. 'Did Jake come up in the truck with you? Did he come to our place? And how did *he* know what had happened? God – I hope it wasn't on the news or something!'

'No, no, there's been nothing said about it anywhere that I'm aware of. But I called a help line on his company's website last night and managed to wrangle his phone number out of them. I had a terrible job persuading them I was genuine.' He grinned. 'I said it was about a close relative who was lost in the bush, and I'd lost his private phone number. His car is at our place.'

'OK, but *why* did you call him in the first place? For God's sake, dad, what a thing to do! You don't even know him.'

'I wanted someone who'd really want to find you to come with me. We were going to start searching if you hadn't been found so quickly. I never ask your uncle for anything if I can help it, you know that. He would have driven me crazy, speculating and telling me non-stop what you should have done or not done the way he always does. I called Ben from the band, but he'd gone straight to Hamilton with his family after the thing in Henderson Park. So, I called Jacob, I had a feeling he wouldn't mind help me find you.'

She stared at him, surprised by this cryptic comment but decided not to comment. The back story to what had made him do this extraordinary thing was something she wasn't prepared to discuss when she was so exhausted. Her eyes closed and she just had time to think, 'Jacob – that must be his real name', then she was asleep.

12

*A*lba woke up when Steve opened the passenger door on the driveway at the house. 'Come on – let's go inside and get you cleaned up, and then you can have a proper sleep in your bed. You look exhausted.'

She got out of the car and looked around, slightly disorientated and yawned. 'Wow, I slept all the way back! I feel a lot better now. Where's Jake?'

'He left right away - said he'd leave us to it. Nice guy!'

'Mm,' said Alba and yawned again. 'Yeah, he's very nice. Let's go inside, I can't wait to get out of these jeans. They feel as if they've dried onto me like a second skin. I'll have to bin them.'

'Why?' asked Steve over his shoulder as he unlocked the front door. 'Can't you just wash them?'

'Dad! They've got pine sap all over them, I peed in them twice and I never want to see them again.'

She closed the door behind her and peeled the jeans off there and then. 'Here,' she said and held them out. 'Only touch the waistband and put them in the rubbish bin, please! I mean it, I'll never put them on again.'

She spent a long time in the shower, scrubbing sap and dirt off herself, standing under the hot water dreamily enjoying the feeling of being warm and clean. Her hands were red and raw, covered in scratches and little puncture wounds, but she managed to get the sticky sap off by using the oil she had taken from the pantry on her way to the bathroom. The first time an Instagram reel turned out really useful, she thought. Not that I thought I'd ever need to clean myself with cooking oil, but I can vouch for it now.

'Sleep first or a late lunch?' Steve looked up and smiled when she came into the kitchen dressed in PJ's and barefoot.

'Oh, definitely something to eat first, I'm starving. I lost my pack when I fell, so I didn't get to eat my lunch – my last meal was yesterday's breakfast. Can you have a look at my shoulder?'

She pulled her top to one side and turned around for him to see. 'Oh, shit,' said Steve quietly and ran his fingers of her shoulder blade. 'That's a terrible bruise. I wonder if you should have an x-ray in case something's broken.'

'It's not serious, it's just a bruise. I think I got hit by a minor boulder when I crashed down that steep slope. There was a lot of debris falling all around me. I haven't told you the whole story yet. But I've got full movement in the shoulder - it's only sore muscles, so let's not fuss about it. I just wanted to know if the skin was broken. It was hard to see.'

Telling the story over a sandwich lunch took time. She tried to keep it on a timeline, so her father would understand how dangerous it had been, how insecure she felt on that swaying branch and how she had managed to get herself into a safe position, inch by inch. But he kept interrupting and asking her to explain things in more detail, until she finally understood what was going on. He didn't have the knack of seeing what she described to him in three dimensions in his mind, something she had never realised before. What a handicap, she thought, not to be able to picture things like live images by hearing them described.

'Hang on, dad, I'll be back in a moment.' She ran down the hallway to her bedroom, picked up a notepad and a pencil and returned to the table.

'I'll draw it for you,' she said. 'Let's move these plates and stuff to one side and then you come and sit beside me. I'm going to make a picture story of this, like a cartoon strip.'

Ten minutes later Steve looked at the row of nine pages she had filled with quick pencil sketches and lined up on the table. 'Amazing!' he said, deeply impressed. 'I haven't seen any drawings of yours for years. I get it now, how you were first caught on that branch and what you had to do to reach a safe spot – you moved like one of those caterpillars. But turning around once you were sitting up! My God – I don't know how you did it! The height of that tree - and how steep the slope was. You must have been terrified.'

He leaned over and pulled her against him, and they sat like that for a moment, then she got up. 'I'll go to bed and sleep for a few hours, and then I must go out and get a new phone. Mine's in my daypack somewhere down in that deep gully, probably buried under rocks and dirt.'

'OK, you do that. I'll tidy up here. What kind of phone was it?'

'Oh, just a common garden variety, nothing fancy. An Oppo, the model with the bigger screen so I could read books on it. It was a great phone - I'll probably get another one just the same.'

Alba woke up from a deep sleep and discovered it was six o'clock and her father had just turned on the TV news, but when she appeared, still in her PJs, he muted to sound.

'I went out and got a new phone for you, it's a later model, but it's the right size and the right make.' He pointed at the table. 'The girl in the shop said if you have trouble retrieving your data from the cloud, whatever that is, just bring it in and she'll do it for you. I showed her what your number was on my phone, and she went out the back and put it into this new phone.'

'What? How did she do that? I didn't know it could be done.'

'Don't ask me,' said her father. 'You know I'm hopeless with that kind of thing. She said she could do it, and she was only gone about ten minutes. I think she said the network had done something remotely, but I don't know how it works. She showed me that the number is the same, though.' He thought for a moment. 'And she said she could have downloaded all your stuff from the old phone and put it on this one from that cloud thing – photos and texts and whatever, but she wasn't allowed to do it and then give the phone to me, against company policy.'

Alba sat down on a chair laughing helplessly. 'Of course, she couldn't – what if you'd started looking through all my text messages and seen the sexy ones, and the *photos*? Heavens, dad! Just thinking about it makes my toes curl.'

'You haven't!' said Steve. 'Please tell me you don't do that sort of thing!'

'Of course, not. I'm not stupid, I'm just kidding. There's nothing there I wouldn't be happy for you to look at, I don't think. And thank you for getting the phone for me!'

Later that evening, after a take-out pizza to replace the one that had gone to waste the night before when Steve realised that something was wrong and left it on the bench to go cold and congeal, his phone pinged several times in rapid succession.

'Well, look at that!' he said excitedly after a few moments. 'What a neat thing to do.' He handed her the phone. 'That park ranger who found you sent a whole raft of photos.'

And there she was, first a nearly hidden little figure concealed by huge branches and then a photo looking down the nearly vertical drop, showing how steep the slope was with the trail of mud and stones disappearing down into the depths of the gully. Then the picture of the helicopter rescue with the man being winched down and how far out he had to swing, then the two of them hanging one below the other in their harnesses, and a final one of her being pulled into the helicopter.

'That tree was even taller than I thought. If I hadn't got caught on that branch, I would probably have continued all the way down that steep slope getting slammed into rocks and trees.'

'I know,' said her father. 'I was thinking just that – and how on earth would they have found you if you had been knocked unconscious?'

'You must thank him from both of us for being so thoughtful,' said Alba. 'And tell him I've never been so pleased to see anyone in my life.'

Amused she watched out of the corner of her eye as Steve spent some time writing and sending the message and thought of course that's how it was. He didn't use his phone much, mostly just to text the band members or her and occasionally to take a photo. It had always been her mother who kept up to date with technical things, who used her phone for nearly everything and knew all the tricks.

'Dad,' she said when he seemed to have finished. 'How old were you and mum when you married.'

'I was a year or two over forty and Mary has just turned twenty-one.' He paused and frowned. 'Listen, I don't know if Mary ever told you the details, but the opposition to me marrying Mary, from both our families, nearly turned our lives into a war zone. Her parents in Korea were totally against it, they just hated the thought of her marrying me. I was too old, I wasn't Korean, I was a mechanic, and she was in her final year of a degree and was supposed to have a year here then go back home. To them it was a disaster for the family, very personal. And my parents and Morgan said it would never last, the age difference was ridiculous, the cultural differences would split us up, it was doomed to fail. We waited until she was twenty-one and got married at the courthouse.'

'But they got over it, didn't they? They saw it was a lasting thing. And if mum hadn't died so young you'd have been happy forever. It was as clear as daylight, anyone who watched you together could see it.'

'They kind of understood it, but for Morgan resentment replaced the anger. You know how he hates being wrong or not having the last word.'

'He's the supremo of pontification,' said Alba and giggled. 'Thinks he knows everything, a global authority on every subject under the sun. Yep, that's my uncle. But what do you mean by resentment? *What* does he resent? The fact that you were both so happy?'

'Having been proved wrong, of course. The longer Mary and I lasted, the more resentful he got, and that made him sarcastic and nasty. Don't forget I've known him a long time and I understand how his mind works.'

Alba got up. 'There's no human kindness in that man, he's beyond help. Do you want a beer? I think I'll celebrate my continued existence by opening a bottle of that lovely wine I bought a couple of weeks ago, the one I tasted at Carla and Blair's place. And I'll have a go at getting all the data back on my phone. I'll turn it on now and get my laptop so I can research how to do it.'

She didn't get round to uploading her phone data, because by the time she had got Steve's beer and poured her own wine, her new phone had already issued several alerts. She picked it up from the table and stared at the screen, but nothing showed, and she realised she would have to set everything up from scratch again, email app, news media apps, social media apps, and all her screen settings. What she had in her hand was just the basic setup Android provided automatically, apart from the alert.

'Dad, did that girl at the shop tell you what she set the lock PIN to?'

'I forgot to say. It's my birthday, not the year, just the day and the month. I told her to do that, so I'd remember it. That's why she wouldn't re-install your stuff. Breach of privacy, she said.'

She had five text messages and opened the folder, but after one look she decided to go and read them in private. She took her glass of wine and retreated to her bedroom and sat on the bed.

'I know your phone was lost, the ranger told Steve, and he told me just now that you have the old number on a new phone. Can't tell you how relieved I am you're OK. J'

'Terrific drawings, you have such varied talents. Don't know how you managed to keep safe in that bloody tree. J'

'Those photos the ranger took are incredible. J'

'How are your hands? J'

'I've got to stop this, but a last one. Please promise you won't go on dangerous treks alone in the future. It's not good for my heart. J'

Alba sent him one reply. *'Can't promise, it's my favourite thing to recharge my batteries. You can come if you want to. Thanks for helping my dad, it was lovely to see you there. A xx'*

She picked up her glass of wine, went back to the living room and made no comment to Steve about all the photos he had sent to Jake. I bet it's the first time ever he's taken photos and sent them, she thought, he must have taken them when I went to have a sleep. And no wonder he spent so long after the ranger sent *his* photos, he wasn't just thanking the rescue guy, he was also forwarding everything to Jake. I hope I'm not going to regret putting those two kisses at the end of my text.

13

Alba ended the call with Jake, put the phone in her back pocket and reached for the box she needed, lowered it in a controlled sliding drop to the platform and took out the part she was looking for and half a dozen more to put in the right place on a lower shelf. Then she wolf-whistled and heard an answering whistle from an aisle somewhere behind her and knew one of the guys would turn up and lift the heavy box back up on the top storage shelf again. They had worked out a system when she first started working there and they realised she was too short and not strong enough to do what they found easy. They had taught her to wolf whistle and teased her about what a useful a skill it would be if she saw some guy she fancied on the other side of the street.

While she continued to pack orders, she refined the ideas that had popped into her head while she talked to Jake, the little tests she could set for herself to define how the dread thing worked. All she needed was one meeting where someone in the room gave her the dread feeling. It might take ages, she thought, or it might never happen at all. Maybe it wouldn't work at one remove, if the bad intensions weren't directed at herself, but it was worth trying.

Throughout the rest of the day thoughts about the upcoming meeting and thoughts about Jake continued to revolve in her head. Maybe there would only be one or two people a year who weren't being straight with Jake, about to scam him or trick him in some way. Or maybe those that had gone wrong in the past never planned their various misdeeds, maybe it was just later they decided to deviate from their contract with Jake. If he wasn't so supportive of the ambitions of others, this would never have become a problem for him. Now that she knew how many he had provided start-up capital for or invested in, she understood why he was so keen to see if she could help him weed out those who might try to take advantage of him. She continued planning exactly how she could carry out her initial test, what to say and how to look and decided not to tell Jake but keep it as surprise and only tell him if it worked.

As planned, they met in a side street, so they could arrive together and make it look as if they had walked or driven together across town from the

MoreIT office. As Jake had said on the phone that morning when they went over the scenario again, 'We've got to think of the details. If you're doing a week of work experience you would have been at the office, so let's make it look right.'

The room just beside the hotel bar was more like a large square alcove, a room with one wall missing, open to the bar itself. Someone had pushed three small, square tables into a long one and arranged six chairs around it and put out water and glasses.

Jake looked around. 'The others organised this room for us. How about we sit down together on the far side, so they have to face us both?'

Alba picked up her satchel put it on the chair on her other side and said, 'Just so they can't sit on this side.'

While pulling out her notebook and her ballpoint pen on the table, Alba didn't notice that Jake had got to his feet and walked towards two men who had just arrived at the far end of the bar. She remained quietly at the table, doodling in her notebook, and tried to look as if she wasn't paying attention, the way she used to do at school. Then a third man arrived, and she heard Jake introduce him to the other two as Gregory, so he was the one Jake trusted.

'And who is this then?' asked the taller of the two who had come in first and smiled at Alba.

'This is Maria Kim, she's doing a work experience with us - and she's doing a special assignment at the same time,' said Jake. 'Observing only, she's not allowed to take part, but she's quite sharp, so don't mention anything commercially sensitive.'

The taller man turned directly to Alba. 'Year 12, are you? Is it business studies? And what's the topic of the assignment?'

'No, I'm in year 13,' said Alba trying to sound shy. 'It's about comparing structured formal meetings with informal ones, and how the various ways of conducting meetings might result in different outcomes. It's called an observational study because you have to draw conclusions from how people say things and respond.'

They all smiled at her, and she thought how funny this was. She was twenty-four years old, and these three men totally believed that she was a schoolgirl.

When they were seated the tall man asked if anyone wanted a drink and got up to order beers for himself and his friend and a grapefruit juice for Alba. She glanced at Jake and Gregory who had declined the offer of drinks and wondered if it was significant in some way, then she closed the notebook and put it and the pen on the chair beside her satchel. She had felt Jake's look when she got them out and knew he probably wondered why she had brought them when the fictitious study was supposed to be observational, but it was part of the plan, and she would tell him later. She sat quietly through the opening explanations from the tall man and glanced around at the faces of the others, presenting the image of an attentive student. After some initial questions from Jake and Gregory and replies from the other two, the taller man got his phone out and aimed it at her and Jake.

'I must get a photo of this,' he said casually, 'it's like you've got a little personal assistant, very cute. I'll put in on Insta so Georgia will see it. My daughter,' he explained to Alba. 'She's a year younger than you, she's in year 12.'

Jake reached across the table and pushed the phone aside. 'No Adam, don't,' he said without sounding urgent. 'She's not supposed to be anywhere without wearing her school uniform – we can't get her into trouble. I had to get special permission to take her with me out of the office and practically swear on a bible that she'd be kept safe, so no photos. If her school finds out she's in a bar and out of uniform, all hell will break out.'

The tall man, who Alba now understood was Jake's friend, not the untidy, shorter one, put the phone to one side and said, 'Sorry, Maria, I didn't think - of course we don't want you to get into trouble at school.'

A few minutes later, when Jake was replying to a question from Adam's friend about hedge funds and the men on the other side of the table were focusing on him, the dread feeling suddenly and powerfully invaded her mind. The vortex of dread took hold of her, making her heart pound and she twitched with discomfort on her chair.

She sent Jake an agonised glance hoping he

would look at her because the feeling of oppressive threat was hard to tolerate when all she wanted to do was run away, then his eyes briefly meet hers and she could feel the unspoken message. 'Keep calm, nothing's going to happen, I'll deal with it.'

A couple of minutes later, while Adam and his friend were explaining something to Gregory, Jake slowly reached for her right hand, which was fisted on her lap and covered it with his hand. But dread overpowered the feeling she usually experienced when he touched her. She knew he was worried about her, and she appreciated the intention, but what if the others noticed? After a few moments she slid her hand out from under his and rested it on the edge of the table.

She managed to sit through an agonising half hour while suggestions and questions went back and forth, notes were made on both sides of the table and the dread feeling surrounded her like a crackling forcefield. When they were gathering up their notes and phones, she jumped to her feet, picked up her satchel and the notebook and met Jake's surprised eyes.

'Sorry,' she said, 'I've got to catch the bus now.' She left without further ado, before any of them had reacted, walked straight through the bar, out to the foyer and then to the street where she spent a couple of minutes working out the best vantage point and waited.

Five minutes later she saw the tall man and his friend through the windows in the bar and met them at a half run as they came out of the door. 'Hey,' said the tall friendly one. 'You're back again, did you miss the bus?'

She gave him her best shy little girl smile and said, 'I left my pen on the chair, so I'll have to take the next bus. I want to make notes about some things I need to look up like that hedge fund thing while I remember them. It sounded interesting, but I don't know anything about it.'

'It is interesting,' said Adam. 'Very interesting and Jake is particularly clever with things like that.'

They smiled and continued, and she stopped in the foyer and watched them walking away. The wait for Jake and Gregory to come out seemed endless, and she was tempted to get her phone out to pass the time, but then she might miss them, so she continued to wait despite curious glances from the reception staff. Finally, the men appeared and went straight outside, and shook hands before Gregory waked away. Jake was looking in both directions, and she pressed Send on the text she had just composed: 'I'm in the foyer, please come back inside.'

She watched him get his phone out and read the text, then he turned and came back inside.

14

She smiled at the look on his face. 'Did you think I'd run away? I'll tell you what I was doing, but it's nearly four now. Let's have a glass of wine – can we?'

They returned to the bar where the barman was tidying up the little open-sided room at the far end and stood at the bar waiting until he noticed them and came across. 'Can I help you?'

'What wine would you like Alba? I'll have a glass of red.'

'Sir, I'm sorry,' said the barman apologetically. 'We can't serve minors, perhaps a glass of juice? If you *are* over eighteen and you show me ID you can have a drink.'

Alba got her driver's license out and showed it to him, he raised his eyebrows and grinned. 'So, what would you like?'

They sat at a round table by the window and Alba waited for the question, but Jake held off until their drinks were delivered. 'I saw what happened in there – I could feel the tension. Who was it, could you tell?'

'Both of them.'

'What? Are you sure? And how could you tell? Wasn't it the short guy with the moustache, Adam's friend? He's the one I was suspicious of.'

'No, definitely both of them.' She could see how troubled he was by this, the way his mouth tensed, and creases appeared between his eyebrows.

'It was like a fog of dread in front of the two of them when they looked at you. It happened when you started explaining about the hedge fund thing they asked about - they first glanced at each other and then both of them looked straight at you. It was intense, very hard to sit through.'

He was thinking for a long while, and she sat silently waiting, because if he believed her this would be devastating for him. He would have to adjust all his ideas about one of his friends, re-evaluate all they had done together and then decide how to act.

Impulsively she reached out and curled her fingers around his. 'I know, I do understand,' she said. 'This is awful for you, and I wish I could change it, but I can't. Maybe you can disregard it or work around it somehow, so you can still be friends? Just stay very alert about anything to do with him.'

'No, I couldn't, it would be impossible,' he said after a moment, decisive again. 'I'll decline their invitation and find a way of putting it, so Adam reads the subtext without me spelling it out – that I no longer trust him. It's a relief in a way. I only said I'd hear them out because it was Adam who asked. It wasn't something I wanted to be involved in.' He gave her fingers a little squeeze. 'Do you understand now why I call you an asset?' His eyes were locked on hers and she could feel how important it was to him that she understood what he was saying. 'I wouldn't have guessed about Adam in a million years – not until it blew up in my face one day in the future. Not that I know what those two had on their hidden agenda, but I was suspicious from the start. I just got the wrong guy.'

'I wish I could tell you more, but that's all I get, that dread thing coming off people like a fog of threat and danger. And I always know which one it is, like I did in that job interview at your office - and today.' She paused. 'Well, it's only happened four or five times or so including today, five I think, but so far I've known who it was each time.'

'Is there any chance the dread thing didn't apply to me?' he said after a moment's thought. 'Could it have been directed at Gregory.'

She needed to think. Could it have been? She realised she was still holding his hand and pulled hers back, put her elbows on the table and clamped her temples between her hands with her head tilted down. Could she tell if it was directed at a specific person, if it wasn't directed at her? Yes, obviously she could, she had definitely felt it was directed at Jake, who had sat beside her, and not at Gregory.

'I don't know how it works,' she said after a while and looked up again. 'I only know that today it was definitely aimed at you, it had nothing to do with Gregory. And don't ask how I know, but I do. It felt bad, very dangerous for you - if it had got any worse I would have thrown myself in front of you to protect you, despite how horrid it was - it was so strong!' He stared at her, she felt his surprise and added more calmly, 'I've never felt it aimed at anyone else before, so this is completely new to me too – it wasn't as strong as that time on the bus, but it was powerful.'

She could never tell him what had popped into her head just then, that maybe she had picked it up because that feeling was directed at him, and somehow he and she were on the same spectrum or wavelength or whatever it might be, and she felt so linked to him that she had felt it. She shook her head at the thought, but the idea persisted, because what else could it be? Over the years she must have been face to face with people who were a threat to someone else in the vicinity, but she had never before picked anything up that she hadn't felt was directed at herself.

Jake thought about what she had said, she could see him putting the facts and ideas together into a whole picture, something that would make sense. 'But it could have been directed at you,' he said after a while. 'Maybe they got worried about you hearing all their ideas and plans.'

'I'll tell you why I left like that,' she said instead of replying, knowing how interested he would be to hear this. 'It wasn't that the dread feeling forced me to go, and thanks for trying to protect me, I felt it when you looked at me – when it first hit me. But I'd planned a little test before we started. So instead of leaving for the bus stop I hung around outside where I would see them coming towards the doors, and then when they were nearly there I kind of ran towards them, so we met nearly in the doorway and they both looked right at me. And there was nothing – no dread at all when they focused just on me.'

He thought for a long time, his gaze without focus, then he said, 'Were they surprised to see you coming back?'

'No, I said I'd left my pen on the chair, though it's actually in my bag. I told them I was planning to make notes about the hedge fund thing on the bus because it was such an interesting thing, and I didn't know anything about it. You know, I tried to kind of recreate what had triggered the dread in the meeting. If they'd been concerned about me talking about what you discussed I think those thoughts would have popped back into their heads when they I told them my little story - and I would have got the dread feeling.'

'That's my girl!' said Jake. 'Smart as! But it's time to go now. I should have brought the car so I could drive you home. The buses will be crowded at this time of the day. Are you going to finish your wine?'

'Crowded buses are part of my life, don't worry. Sometimes I don't drink more than half a glass though I like wine, because I've got what they call "the Chinese gene" – well, I've partly got it. My body doesn't produce quite enough of that enzyme that breaks down alcohol, so my tolerance level is low. I can always tell when I must stop.'

And then she remembered that she wanted to thank him and said, hoping she wasn't blushing, 'And thanks for trying to calm me in there – when you took my hand. It was kind of you, and for anything else but dread it would have worked. But dread is stronger than everything, and I don't think it can't be tempered or deflected.'

'It's a force of nature,' said Jake. 'I can't imagine how you lasted as long as you did.'

All she wanted now was to get home and think hard about her many conflicting thoughts and ideas. Outside on the pavement they paused for a moment before going in opposite directions, vaguely discussed a date for another meeting over coffee and then, as Alba turned to leave, a voice spoke right next to her, and she swung back. An elegant blond woman in a bright red coat was looking past her at Jake with a wide smile.

'Jake, darling!' she said exuberantly. 'Fancy

finding you here at this time of the day – are you heading inside for a drink?'

Alba remained where she was, her eyes on Jake, who was now telling the woman he had to go back to the office for a meeting, then he turned to Alba, reached out and put his arm over her shoulders and pulled her close to his side for a brief moment.

'It was good to see you again, Alba, and thanks for helping. I'll see you soon.'

The woman in the red coat glanced at Alba and said dismissively, 'Yes, you run along, now!' and immediately turned back to Jake again.

Alba spent most of the bus ride home thinking of what had taken place at the hotel, her total certainty that Jake had been the object of the dread feeling, and how much she wished she could read his thoughts, not just some of his emotions. Speculation about the woman in the red coat was pushed to one side, too full of pitfalls and contradictions to indulge in so soon. She would agonise about it later, in private instead of surrounded by commuting strangers.

15

On Sunday morning when Alba and Steve had just gone out the front door to go to the cemetery Steve's phone buzzed. He pulled his phone out of his jacket pocket and said, 'I'd better take this,' and took a couple of steps to the side.

Alba took his key out of the lock and walked towards the car and heard her father say, 'I've no idea what you're talking about. Why don't you ask Alba – I suppose you have her number. Sorry, I've got to go, the light just turned green.'

He turned to Alba and said quickly, 'I don't know what Morgan's on about, but just to warn you quickly in case he calls. He's seen a photo of you on some news website with a guy and he wants to find out more. Is it you and Jake or that American?'

There was no time to reply; her phone was already signalled a call and on the screen it said Morgan.

'Hi uncle Morgan,' said Alba. 'How are you?'

'Well, aren't you a lucky girl!' said her uncle in a tone of voice that many would have taken objection to, but Alba was used to him and tried not to let his condescension grate on her. 'I couldn't believe my eyes when I saw that photo on the Stuff website just now.'

'I don't know what you've seen,' said Alba. 'I haven't been on the Stuff site this morning. We're just about to go and put flowers on mum's grave – it's her birthday today. I'm just waiting for dad to come back and pick me up.'

Steve was watching her closely and she winked at him.

'Check it out,' said Morgan. 'But fancy a girl like you going out with someone like Tobin!'

'Here's dad, I've got to go, bye!' said Alba and ended the call before she joined her father who had remained standing beside the car and watched her talking to her uncle with a look of disbelief.

'We're a pair of liars,' he said and laughed. 'But we got out of it in record time and it's first time in ages I've got away without a lecture or some nonsense. What's he on about?'

'He's seen something on the Stuff website, I'll have a look and see what he's so excited about while you drive to the florist.'

A few minutes later she groaned and said, 'Oh, shit!' under her breath. 'Someone's posted a couple of photos of me and Jake on Twitter and there's a screenshot of the Twitter post in an article about MoreIT.'

'And?' asked Steve. 'What does the Twitter post say and where did the photos come from?'

Instead of replying to his question, Alba continued to look at her phone for a moment and said, 'It's OK, I think. The article isn't headed up in a way that would make most people open it to read the whole thing. Businesspeople would, I suppose, but not anyone else. The headline is, MoreIT set to announce record dividend Which is OK, and the Twitter post is way down in the article, you'd have to scroll right down to see it. Most people wouldn't read that far.'

Steve said again, 'And? Come on, Alba, tell me what it says – and where were those photos taken?'

'Someone snapped us after the meeting I went to with Jake to the other day. One is taken from outside the window of the bar at the hotel where the meeting was. It's pretty blurry, but when you see me with my hair up in a topknot in the second photo taken when we were outside on the street, you can tell it was us in the bar as well. I'll show you when we stop.'

When she passed her phone to Steve he looked at the images and then at Alba. 'Were you two having a drink and then … and who's that woman on the edge of the second photo? Is she part of the scene or just a passer-by?'

Alba undid her seatbelt and swung around in her seat, so she could face her father full-on. 'We had the meeting with three guys in a room just off the bar that they had booked. And then, when they left, Jake and I had a glass of wine and discussed what I had picked up.'

'So, you did pick up something? Was it the dread thing?'

'I'll tell you about it later, dad. It's a bit of a story. Let's go in and buy some flowers now.'

While the shop assistant wrapped a bouquet of red roses and while ox-eye daises which had been Mary's favourite flowers, Alba stood to one side and studied the photos again. The first one taken through the window showed her and Jake in profile, simply talking across a table, so not very interesting. The second was probably taken from across the street and was of her standing beside Jake with his arm across her shoulders, and it looked as if he had stood like that for some time with Alba close to his side, when it had really just been for a few seconds.

On the way to the cemetery, she texted Jake and said to check to photos and he replied nearly straight away, 'Not worried, just looks like I was being a bit inappropriate with a schoolgirl. If anyone comments I'll say you're the daughter of my friend Steve.'

And then a few seconds later. 'Are you worried about it?'

She replied, 'Not at all, just thinking of you.'

The cemetery was quiet and peaceful with only a few people in sight and nobody anywhere close to

Mary's grave. Alba left her father holding the flowers and took the withered bouquet to the skip over on the far side of the cemetery, rinsed the tall spike vase and brought it back full of water. When she got back she could tell that Steve had cried, but as he unwrapped the flowers and put them into the vase she had pushed deep into the grass, he said quite calmly, 'What are you going to say to Morgan when he calls again?'

'Do you think he'll call again? He didn't say that to me. Mind you, I didn't give him much time to say anything.'

Steve gave her a wry sideways glance. 'Of course, he'll call again. He never lets up until he's got every single thing sorted out in his stubborn mind. So, what are you going to tell him?'

'Certainly not the truth, dad!' Alba laughed and turned to face her mother's gravestone. 'Sorry mum! This is obviously the day for me and dad to tell lots of lies. I'm going to brush him off somehow, preferably with something that drives him crazy - it will come to me when I hear his voice. He brings out the worst in me, every time.'

Alba's uncle called when they were about to have lunch, and she made a face and turned the speaker on so Steve could hear.

'Hi Morgan,' she said. 'I've decided I'm old enough to skip the "uncle" now. What can I do for you?'

Steve stopped with his hand on the fridge door and turned to look at her. She knew he was waiting with bated breath for something either funny or too cheeky. Alba had a history of going a bit too far when baiting her intrusive uncle, and this might turn out to be one of those times.

'So, how does a girl like you know Tobin? I can't imagine you have anything in common with a man like him!'

'Oh, Jake!' said Alba casually. 'Are you calling about him *again*? For heaven's sake, Morgan, what does it matter to you how I know him?'

'I'm interested,' said Morgan briefly. 'So, how well do you know him?'

'I know him *very* well,' said Alba. 'We're good friends and we meet for coffee and lunch now and then. I'm very fond of him, he's a lovely guy. We have fun together.'

'What the hell does that mean? Is he using you?'

Alba adopted her super serious adult tone of voice and said firmly, 'Morgan – now listen *very* carefully to what I'm telling you! What I do or don't do with my friends is absolutely no business of yours. And I'd appreciate it if you could refrain from sneaky slurs on my character and morals. You're often offensive and rude, but today you've seriously overstepped the mark and I'm ending this call right now.'

'Bloody hell!' said Steve, looking stunned and still frozen in place with his hand on the half-open fridge door which was now beeping. 'I bet nobody's ever told him off like that in his whole life.'

'It needed doing,' said Alba and reached for the electric jug which had just boiled. 'He's nearly intolerable and nobody ever faces up to him properly. I'm sick of the way he manages to insult people in that sneaky way by implication, he never says anything straight out. Are you going to get the milk out or do I have to push you to one side and get it myself?'

'But seriously,' said her dad and handed her the milk. 'I've never heard you sound like that before – very impressive. I'm proud of you!'

'Oh, good!' Alba laughed and took their mugs to the table. 'I was hoping you wouldn't object, but I thought laying down some ground rules might be good for him after all these years of him throwing his weight around and terrorising everyone in the family.'

'Now for another touchy subject,' said Alba when they were clearing the table after lunch. 'Could you please put this bowl in the dishwasher? I think it's time we sorted out mum's things, don't you? I mean her make-up and her clothes. There are some things I'd like to keep and probably you want to keep a few things as well, but a lot of it could go to the charity shop, I think.'

She held her breath and continued wiping the table because she didn't want to see his face right then and desperately hoped he wasn't going to cry because that would make her cry too.

'You're right,' said Steve after a long pause. 'We can't put it off forever. What is it you want to keep?'

With an internal sigh of relief, she went to rinse the sponge and said over the sound of running water, 'I want to keep all her Korean things and the dress she got married in and another couple of things that are special.'

'The pink dress? Is it still there?'

'Oh yes, didn't you know? It's on a hanger inside a plastic bag at the back of her wardrobe. When she was ill, while she could still get out of bed, she showed me. She told me you bought it to get married in because you got married in the registry office and you liked her in pink. She made me try it on and said I could use it if I wanted to.'

'I had no idea!' Steve smiled. 'Yes, we bought it together, I waited outside fitting rooms in three shops, I think, before we found the perfect dress. Fancy her keeping it all this time. Did it fit you?'

'Perfectly, it could have been made for me. And it's very pretty in a retro way, totally mid-century with the full skirt and a low scoop neckline, so you two must have liked that look too. I don't think that style ever looks comical like some other old styles do. Very feminine and flattering.'

Much to her surprise Steve asked no further questions about the photos of her and Jake or what the Twitter post had said. While they emptied her mother's wardrobe and sorted things into piles on one side of the bed, some to be discarded and some to go to the charity shops, Alba kept expecting him to bring it up again. By the time they had finished sorting, discussing and making decisions, the afternoon was nearly gone, and the bedroom looked like a disaster zone and Steve had asked nothing more about the photos. Vert unusual, thought Alba and glanced at him where he stood considering the piles on the bed – he usually wants all the details.

'I had no idea so much stuff could come out of one wardrobe and six drawers,' said Steve. 'I'll put the things for the charity shop on the back seat of the car. The rubbish sack can go out with the collection on Tuesday. Let's have a look at what you're keeping.'

Alba pulled one item at a time from the little pile on the chair by the window. 'I'll keep the pink dress, of course, and mum's *hanbok*. It's so elegant and I like that her mother chose one in mauve and white and pink, nothing too bright or patterned. I used to know how to put all the parts on, mum showed me years ago, but I think I'd better check it on the internet if I want to wear it. It's all so specific and I'd have to get it right – even the way the front single-loop bow is tied so the loop faces the right way. Why didn't she wear it to your wedding?'

'I don't know,' said Steve, and it was clear he had never thought of it before now. 'I didn't know she had it until after we were married when she dressed up in it one evening – I think it was our first wedding anniversary. It might have been that she didn't feel it would fit with being married like we did, very simple and low key. Her parents sent it to her when she graduated. They couldn't come for some business reason, so they sent the hanbok.'

'It really is gorgeous,' said Alba who had unzipped the hanbok bag to look at it. 'I hadn't noticed until now that it's the slightly more modern version with the waist nearly at waist level.' She put her hand into the bag and tweaked the hanbok skirt. 'And look, it hasn't got the big, gathered skirt that makes women look as wide as they're tall either, it's got wide folds from the waist, so the skirt will hang nearly straight down. I must wear it sometime for a special occasion.'

She picked up the zipped bag the hanbok was stored in, a large square bag designed with multiple hangers inside for the different parts of the Korean traditional dress and little pockets for the embroidered shoes and white socks. Carrying it by its external hanger she took it to her room and pushed her clothes to one side so it would fit. It's a treasure, she thought, a real heirloom and my halmeoni would have chosen it so carefully, probably from some super expensive place, but she made a great choice.

When Steve returned from the car after a final armful of clothes, she looked around his bedroom, the one that had been her parents' room since the day they moved in a few months before she was born.

'What are you going to put in that wardrobe now? You haven't got enough clothes to fill it.'

'Don't you worry! I thought of that while I've taken things to the car. I'll keep my band uniform and my saxophone plus my winter jackets and boots there instead of in the guest room wardrobe. Much more convenient. Should we have take-aways tonight instead of cooking? I think we deserve it and we haven't had any for ages.'

They had Thai take-out food for dinner and watched two episodes of a new Netflix series, and though Alba twice looked at text messages on her phone, to her surprise no questions or comments about the photos of her and Jake emerged, and she went to bed, intrigued by this unexpected lack of curiosity.

16

Since the meeting with Adam at the hotel, Alba had heard from Jake now and then, mostly by text. Just short messages asking how she was, but nothing new had come up where he needed her help. Soon after the meeting at the hotel Alba had asked if declining Adam's offer had worked out all right. She had thought about the difficulty a lot, how Jake would say he wasn't interested and also manage to convey the impression that he was suspicious. But when she asked, he only replied that it had gone well, and he would tell her the details next time they met, but no suggestion about meeting for coffee had come for a few weeks.

When Alba realised that her father hadn't been in touch with the bank about paying off the mortgage sooner, she was exasperated. 'But you said you would! Let's do it now so we can start reducing the balance a bit quicker. Money is accumulating in my account and it's going nowhere.'

'I hate dealing with the bank,' said Steve reluctantly with a guilty expression that made Alba smile. 'Mary always did it and she knew how to put things – I'm not comfortable doing it.'

Alba could see he was being honest, though it surprised her. It was yet another thing she had never realised about her father, but thinking back she could see that her mother's smart and practical mind had simply taken over all the difficult tasks and removed them from his shoulders.

'OK, let's go together then. I can't change things, because the loan isn't in my name, but if we go together we should be able to sort it out, don't you think?'

The meeting with the loan manager at Steve's bank threw up an obstacle Alba hadn't predicted. She told him there was a sizeable monthly payment coming into her account with an ever-increasing credit balance and got out her phone to show him. She explained that she had a full-time job in a warehouse, for which she was paid fortnightly, and that the much larger monthly payment was for a private consultancy contract which would run for four years. The look on the man's face made her first cringe, then smoulder with anger.

'No,' she said firmly and looked him in the eye. 'I am *not* paid by a brothel or by some man to be his stand-by sex toy or to lend to other businessmen. I have a talent for spotting fraud which is used only rarely, but they want me to be available at short notice when they need me, so they pay me a large monthly retainer.'

'And what if this contract doesn't last for four years?' said the loan manager, who had visibly flinched when she stared him down. 'Will your father be able to keep up the repayments? Or if you decide you want that money for yourself and stop helping him out?'

Alba thought fast about options and ways to get through this without involving Jake, but there was no way of ensuring it would work unless she asked him to vouch for her. In her mind the idea of getting rid of the mortgage had taken on a huge importance, and it had to happen, whatever she had to do to achieve it, even if that meant possibly humiliating herself.

'Listen carefully,' she said, put her phone on the desk and pointed. 'This number here is the number to Jacob Tobin, the CEO of MoreIT which I'm sure you've heard about. It's the number for his personal phone. I'll Google the company number and ask to talk to him if he's in the office, or if he's out I'll ask his secretary, whose name is Elizabeth, to confirm to you that the number is genuine, then I'll call him so you can talk to him yourself.'

The manager tried to avoid this by continuing to talk about how her assurance that she would continue to assist in paying off her father's mortgage was hard to lock in place, so in the end, Alba held her hand up, palm out. He stopped talking and watched as she found the MoreIT number on the Internet.

She dialled the company number and put the phone on speaker. With the phone on the table between her and the loan manager, she asked for Elizabeth and said briskly, 'Hi, Elizabeth, it's Alba. I don't know if Jake has mentioned the contract he has with me as a project consultant, but I need to verify for someone that the number I have on my phone is his personal one, and that I'm employed by him. I'm at the bank with my dad reorganising a mortgage and I need to speak to Jake.Or is he available now?'

'Oh, hi Alba,' said Elizabeth, and Alba could hear the smile in her voice. 'Yes of course, I know who you are. He's gone out for lunch, but you can call him if you need to talk to him. I think he's gone out on his own.'

'OK, did he explain to you why he's given me this contract?'

'Yes, he said he's using you as a truth filter, whatever that means, but I know you're a valuable asset, if I can call you that. He told me recently that you've been very useful once already. If you read out the number you need to verify, I'll tell you if it's Jake's personal number.'

A minute later they ended the call and Alba dialled Jake's cell phone. 'Hi Jake,' she said when he answered. 'Dad and I are at the bank trying to change the mortgage I told you about, the one I want to help him pay off. I've got the phone on speaker. Can you please confirm for the loan manager here that you're not paying me to be your sex toy or something?'

'What?! Did they suggest that?'

'Not in so many words, but I could read his mind.' She smiled at how outraged Jake had sounded and avoided looking at the loan manager's face. 'And could you also confirm the contract isn't going to suddenly cease next month or whatever – my pay, I mean.'

'The contract is for four years and may last longer,' said Jake firmly, sounding like the powerful CEO he was. 'Ask them to set up a direct debit from your account to the loan account – that should keep them happy. How long has the loan got to run?'

'Quite long as it is now, but I'd like to pay it off in two years, if we can ramp up the repayment rate.'

'OK, can you pass the phone to that manager, please - and mute the speaker first?'

Alba did what he asked and slid the phone across the table, sat back and smiled at her father, who seemed stunned and didn't smile back. She fixed her gaze on the manager's face while he listened to Jake for a surprisingly long time without saying a single word; she would have loved to hear what Jake was saying. Finally, Jake stopped talking and the manager said, 'Yes, of course, we can do that, Mr Tobin, no trouble. There's no need for you to personally guarantee it, none at all. Thank you!'

'It's all sorted,' he said and handed Alba's phone back 'No need to do anything more. I'll have the new loan contact drawn up and emailed to you, sir. All you need to do it sign it and return it to us. Which means that the loan will be fully repaid in twenty-four months.'

As they walked back to the car Steve put his hand on her shoulder and gave her a little squeeze. 'That's the second time you've shown me this amazingly decisive, not to say stroppy, personality I never knew about before. I'm so proud of you – you're just like Mary was.'

17

After a brief exchange of messages when Alba thanked Jake for intervening in the mortgage negotiations and told him how it had worked out, she heard nothing from him for another three weeks and missed him enormously, far more than she had expected. To start with she had just quietly looked forward to their next meeting, then it had turned into a vague longing, hoping he would call or text soon and ask to meet. Now she felt as if an important part of her life was absent, some kind of fixed point or an undefined link to something vital that she tried not to think about.

Whenever she thought of Jake she would also wonder at herself and how she had dared be so cheeky and behave like a naughty child right from the start.

'It was that tiny twitch at the corner of his mouth, and the way I felt I knew him already,' she whispered to herself, as she taped up another box of parts, stuck the label on and put it at the end of her trolley.

These whispered conversations she had with herself had evolved out of nowhere since she hadn't heard from Jake. For some reason hearing the words spoken made her feel how true her feelings for Jake were, that they were based on something real, not just imagined. It was like telling a friend something in confidence, and though she still didn't quite understand why she continued doing it, she took comfort from it. It's better than just thinking silently about it, she told herself and it makes me acknowledge to myself that what I feel is genuine, that I'm not fantasising.

'And even if that little tweak hadn't been there,' she continued as she reached for the tablet to check the details of the next order, 'I would have known pretty soon that there was another side to him, because within minutes of meeting him I felt totally safe teasing him. I felt I knew him so well already, as if we'd known each other forever. And now I feel very lonely.'

Over the years she had had various short-term boyfriends, and then Will who lasted more than a year, but she had never felt the slightest inclination to make anything permanent out of it. She had continued to live at home and then Will, the boyfriend at the time, had given up on her when she left her studies and took on being the fulltime caregiver for her mother. Even now, more than two years later, she felt a spurt of anger at the way he had utterly failed to understand that caring for her dying mother had to be her first concern. 'Surely you can leave her with your dad and come the Brent's party!' he had said impatiently. 'Can't he look after her for the night?'

The third or fourth time they had this conversation, she broke the relationship off. Her mother needed nearly constant attention by then, and Alba slept with her bedroom door open for several months, so she could hear if her mother needed her, having dispatched her father to the guest room, so he would get some rest and be able to carry on working.

She became an expert caregiver and learnt to cope with the sometimes unpleasant needs of a patient who reacted badly to both chemotherapy and radiation treatment. During the last couple of months of her mother's life Alba knew exactly how to judge when to give another dose of morphine rather than wait the prescribed four hours, to avoid putting her mother through the torment of the previous dose wearing off. She got used to sights and smells that at the start had made her gag and had once or twice made her vomit. She spent the final two weeks of her mother's life at her bedside, never once going outside the property.

The warehouse job came about by chance when she overheard a conversation at the local supermarket shortly after her mother's funeral, left without the milk she had come for, and drove straight over to the Penrose industrial area and got the job on the spot. When she told her father she had a job he was disappointed and told her it was silly not to go back to university and finish her degree when she had only a year left, but Alba knew she needed a period of complete change, a new routine would be a breathing space.

'I can't go back to uni just yet,' she had told him. 'I need to do something physical and basically mindless for a while and have a change – like a factory reset. And then I'll go back and finish my degree and do something clever and earn pots of money. Don't worry, I'm not abandoning my plans forever, this is just a year's delay.'

She couldn't tell him that she worried about their finances, but early on she had noticed how her mother's long illness had impacted on their lives. As a successful accountant, Mary had always been the highest earner, and when she became too ill to work some aspects of their lives had been discarded as unnecessary luxuries. When Alba gave up her own part-time student job in a burger shop to care for her mother, she had, without consulting either of her parents, changed their shopping habits a little and cut back on some of the more expensive items they had always enjoyed, apart from the foods her mother could still tolerate. To go back to her studies and use money instead of earning it had seemed like a bad idea. What she would earn from the warehouse job was not much above the minimum wage, but it helped with the household budget, which was all she cared about for the time being.

But now things were different, the financial worry had been removed, only to be replaced by Alba's personal worry about Jake. One evening she decided that she simply must work it out and try to determine if her instincts were wrong, and if her imagination was over-riding her common sense. She lay awake for a long time, going over things in her mind, trying to find something that might be a definitive clue to how Jake regarded her. Over the last few months there had been a few things that in retrospect seemed ambiguous, and she listed them in her head, scrutinised them and tried to assess each one on its merits.

The time he told her to just carry on training him and called her a nasty little bully – had his voice held a tone of real affection or just a note of teasing to match hers? When he held her so close after she told him about the man on the bus, had he felt that elusive current she had been so aware of, or had it been a one-sided sensation on her part? Had she imagined that she felt his body react to hers? The way he had anchored her against him as if he couldn't bear for her to be distressed; was it kindness or something deeper? And his reaction in the regional park when she got out of the helicopter. The way his fingers had dug into her shoulders when he took hold of her, and how his eyes were so intense when he asked if she was hurt. It had felt significant even at the time, not just in retrospect, she thought, as she lay there with her eyes closed, reliving the moment. The way he said "that's my girl" when she teased him about not wanting to lose an asset. Somehow it felt special, not so much the words, but how spontaneous it was and the tone of his voice, but then he stepped back quite abruptly, as if he felt he had gone too far or revealed too much. But perhaps the most significant thing was how he had asked her to promise she would never change. She could see his face in her mind, the way he had looked straight into her eyes as if her answer held some special importance, and the feeling it had given her later when she thought about it. The memory was infused with significance, like an indication of something she couldn't put her finger on, something that might hold the key to her frustrating doubts.

Alba went through her list of little incidents over and over without reaching a conclusion and decided that if there were no further clues to help clarify things, she would have to be very careful. There was a disturbing possibility in the back of her mind, that he did feel both kindness towards her and attraction, but just a sexual attraction, not romantic or lasting. Maybe he was in a relationship already and would never act on his possible desire for Alba. Or he might just feel friendly affection for her. Her thoughts went from one possibility to another without reaching any conclusion. The thought of her losing what he might see as only an affectionate and casual working relationship was too much to contemplate. She must be careful to not reveal what she felt and give no hint of how much she wanted him to show he was interested in her or how attractive she found him. If she embarrassed him or made him feel he acted inappropriately she might ruin their strange partnership.

When she finally slept she dreamed of being in the tree, relived vividly how insecure she had felt before she worked out how to struggle in towards the safely of the tree trunk, and then her dream changed. Now she was struggling, losing her grip, then she was falling fast with branches smashing against her face and body, and she screamed. Waking up with a sudden jerk, instantly fully awake, she lay panting, still caught in the dream. Slowly she calmed down and her body relaxed. There was no sound in the house, so she hadn't woken her father. Maybe that scream had just been part of the dream and not a real scream. It took a long time to go back to sleep with her mind alternating between thinking about the dream and continuing to worry about Jake.

It was only when she woke up in the morning that she began to wonder if her teasing, and how Jake had thought she was a teenager the first time they met, meant that he subconsciously continued to regard her as very young, too young to take a real interest in, even though he knew her real age now.

And in that case, all the little incidents she had tried to analyse last night could have been based on the initial impression of her age, and he had simply let her play her bully game and comforted her when she was upset the way he would have with a child. She sighed, flung the covers back and went to have a shower, feeling more conflicted and uncertain than she ever had in her life.

18

When Alba went to have a cup of coffee at mid-morning on the Monday, she had no idea that her world would soon change abruptly. She met Mark in the doorway to the staff room, and he pointed at the table and said, 'I brought in the weekend paper if you want to have a look. I think the boys have finished with it, so put it in the recycling bin when you've read it.'

Alba discarded the sections that were of no interest, read the news section and at the end of her break took the weekend magazine with her along with her lunchtime sandwich and her water bottle. Sometimes she preferred to stay in the aisle she was working in and sit quietly on her trolley leaning against a pile of boxes reading, and today was one of those days. At midday she made herself comfortable, unwrapped her sandwich and picked up the weekend magazine. Idly flicking through it and noting that the amount of advertising far outstripped any editorial content, she turned a page and found herself looking at a photo of Jake and a striking looking woman in a low-cut, tight orange dress and very high heels. The picture had been taken at an award presentation for para-athletes and the caption read "Samantha Tobin, well-known supporter of para-athletics with MoreIT CEO Jake Tobin."

In the space of a second Alba's mind turned into a dark pit of doubt, and for a moment she thought she might cry, she choked back a sob and sat staring down at the photo without really seeing it. Her thoughts from the night now seemed ridiculous, like castle built in the air with no foundation. She told herself that she hadn't lost anything, that you can't lose what you never had, but she failed to convince herself. She really did feel she had lost something precious, nearly tangible; something with no name and no clear definition. She told herself that the feeling that she had a strong emotional link to Jake had fooled her into thinking he might also care for her, and she must stop dwelling on it and be sensible.

When Ludo texted and asked her to go to a movie that night, she said she was busy, but she would be up for a lunch on Saturday, thinking that seeing him in the daytime would remove any repetition of that abrupt grab he had made after the dinner date. She knew her decision to say yes to another date was perverse, she didn't like him and they had nothing in common and wondered why she had done it. Probably a silly thing to do, she thought as she pushed the Warthog across the central aisle to the Peugeot section and started climbing to find the right shock absorbers for a Hastings garage who wanted the branded product. Now she must keep from knee-jerk responses when she was with Ludo, even if against the odds he tried to get her to come back to his flat even in the middle of the day. But no compensation-sex would be on offer and no kisses either, all she had to do was stay friendly and focused and repel any further grab manoeuvres.

When Alba got home from her date Steve was sitting at the table with a shoebox and the big album her mother had kept in front of him.

'Did you have fun?' he asked without looking up, his hands full of photos he was sorting into little piles.

'No, I didn't have fun,' said Alba. 'I don't know why I went out with him again, he's basically boring and he's also a borderline misogynist. And he's not got an atom of fun or nonsense in him, he's so serious he should re-train as a funeral director.'

Steve glanced at her and said calmly, 'You sound like someone who needs a cup of coffee or some ice cream. Remember how Mary always used to say that those two things would nearly always make you feel better?'

'Ice cream, I think. Do you want some?'

'No, I had some earlier, but there's enough left for you. I'll get some more tomorrow. Did he make a pass at you?'

'He nearly mauled me – at lunchtime! - but I got away undamaged. He's not just too serious, he's also totally without intuition or understanding or whatever it is you need to understand that when someone says "no" they mean it. He certainly never heard of the unconditional no. He's clever and stupid at the same time.' She sat down opposite her father and studied the little piles of photos spread over half the table. 'What are you doing? Are you looking for something?'

'I thought it would be nice to have the photo of Mary and you in a frame, the one I took at the afternoon concert on the Domain when you were four or five – the one we went to with a couple from Mary's office and their kids. I always liked it, but it doesn't seem to be here.'

'Oh yes, I remember that day - and the boy had a nosebleed. I can still remember how scary I thought it was when I saw blood coming out of his nose. Isn't it on your phone?'

'No, it was before the smartphone era, I think, or at least I didn't have one, so it must be a print I'm remembering. I thought if it wasn't in the album it would be in the box, but I can't find it.'

They spent a few minutes looking through the prints again and then Alba said, 'Of course, it's not here. I know where it is – I'll get it.'

She left him and returned from the living room

with her mother's lacquered box inlaid with mother-of-pearl that always sat on the side table.

'This is where it is.' She put the box on the table and opened it, and there was the photo, stuck to the inside of the lid. 'I remember seeing this once when I opened the box to show Linley the norigae. I bet mum put the photo there because it's a box about her and me - the norigae is a woman's ornament.'

She lifted out the long silk norigae tassel with the elaborate spherical knot holding the silk threads together and the filigree silver fitting at the top, where the loop started. 'If I ever get married I want to wear this, just like mum did at your wedding. She told me it had been her grandmother's.'

Steve took it from her and held it up. 'You'll have seen it in the photo from the registry office. She wore the pink dress and had this pinned in her hair.' He gave the norigae a little shake to make the long strands of silk swing. 'Like having a family member present at the wedding you could say. I don't know if it was supposed to be on her head, but that's what she did.'

Alba hesitated, but now might be the perfect moment to finally ask the question she had never found the right moment for. 'You know the day I called you and said she had fallen unconscious, and could you come home right away?'

'God yes, I'll never forget that day,' said Steve sadly. 'Racing home like a maniac through the traffic and then getting here ten minutes too late. It broke my heart.'

They were silent for a few moments, then Alba said quietly, 'There was something else that day, but I haven't told you before.' She hesitated, but she knew that now she had started, she had to continue. 'Just before she lost consciousness mum said something that I've never been able to make sense of. She looked at me and said, "I'm so glad *you* are safe from this". Then she closed her eyes and I have no idea what she meant, and she never opened her eyes again.'

'Was that all she said? She didn't explain?' Steve shook his head. 'It must have been the morphine - you know how she would lose track of a conversation and kind of drift off? She would have meant the test she commissioned to be done on your DNA.'

'I didn't know I had a DNA sample taken!' exclaimed Alba, but a moment later she did recall it. 'You mean when I was at primary school, eight or nine perhaps? When we all did that inside cheek swab thing and mum sent them off. I hadn't thought of that in years. Why did we do that?'

'We did it out of curiosity - friends of ours had done it and found out some very surprising things about their genetic background, lots of random traces. So, we thought we'd do it too.'

Alba still didn't see the connection. 'But how did it make me safe?'

Steve gave her a wry smile. 'When Mary was diagnosed with pancreatic cancer her father told her that he thought it ran in the family on his side, that she might have been genetically disposed to it. So, a bit down the track Mary started worrying about you in case you had inherited it, and then eventually she asked for your genome to be re-examined for the hereditary gene. The company that did the original testing keeps each person's data and they have a website where you can order additional stuff, even years later. We got the result a month or so before she died. She really wanted to know you didn't carry that gene, and you don't. But she wanted to tell you herself, and I thought she had, so I never mentioned it.'

$\mathcal{A}$ week later, on a damp, grey Thursday morning the warehouse felt chilly and draughty. Alba was feeling dull and bored as she studied her list of orders, working out how to reduce the number of times she would move from one aisle to another. When her phone buzzed she took the call while still studying the list and felt a frown form on her face when she heard Jake's voice. Now she must be careful, keep her voice neutral and remember that this was possibly about another job, he was her boss, and she was not entitled to those feelings of whatever it was that had percolated through her mind like a grey mist nearly every waking hour for over a week since she saw that picture.

'We need to have a chat about a dinner I'd like you to come to on Saturday, if you have time,' said Jake. 'The dinner date has just been confirmed, or I'd have warned you earlier. Can you come into town this evening? We'll go and have a Japanese dinner and I'll drop you home afterwards. I want to have plenty of time to discuss strategy.'

'I can't come in tonight. I'm cooking dinner for a couple of my dad's friends. It's the first time he's invited anyone over for a long time and I said I'd shop on the way home and cook something nice.'

'That's OK, so how about tomorrow? In town? It might be better than tonight actually.'

His voice had a note of insistence, which wasn't like him, and she felt slightly alarmed. What could be so special about this dinner that they needed extra time to discuss it? Not that she didn't want to see him, she very much wanted to be near him again, but there was something he was hesitating about saying; she felt it like a cold draft on the back of her neck.

'Of course, tomorrow's fine,' she said now. 'The same place as the first time? It's quite near your office, which is good. Any time suits me, I'll just ask for the morning or the afternoon off.'

'Could you possibly take a whole day off? Or from eleven anyway. We might need a bit of time. If your boss doesn't like it, we'll make it afternoon only.'

'What's going on? You sound strange. Is something wrong?'

'No, not really. I'm just a bit embarrassed about what I'm going to ask you to do in case I'm being too demanding.'

Alba made a snap decision to try to bring this

back to the way she normally talked to him, to re-establish what she had felt so comfortable with before. 'Listen Mr Boss-person,' she said, mock-severe, trying hard to sound the same as always, though the words nearly caught in her throat. 'You're paying me a huge salary for doing practically nothing, so you can be as demanding as you like. Do you want me to seduce someone?'

'Shit, no! Absolutely not! Are you crazy? But I need to … no, I'll tell you tomorrow. I think we need to talk about it face-to-face.'

'Ok, see you tomorrow at eleven at the cafe.'

Alba put her phone in her back pocket, then nearly instantly realised what it must be and thought how stupid she had been, it was as clear as daylight. He wanted her to do one last job for him because probably his wife had demanded he stop employing her. Of course, she thought, she's found out, or he's told her that we meet at various places and have coffee and stuff, and now she's getting suspicious or jealous or something, and he's going to terminate the contract, this dinner thing is the last time. Or perhaps she saw those photos in the Stuff article, that wouldn't have helped. That's what he wants to tell me face-to-face. He wants to explain and maybe apologise, and it will go on and on, and it will be agonising and embarrassing, and I'll probably cry.

Her heart sank at the thought, and her busy brain instantly started working out how many more hours she would need to work in some secondary job in order to contribute enough to the mortgage payments. She might not be able to earn enough to pay for the full half the household expenses and she would have zero spending money, but she could probably earn just enough for them to keep up the weekly bank payments. The thought of going back to that mortgage manager at the bank made her cringe. How he would love it if her income suddenly disappeared, and they had to ask for another change. Somehow she must find a second job as fast as she could. *I can do sixty hours a week all up*, she told herself, *anyone can do that. Forty hours here and twenty somewhere else, evenings or weekends, of course I can do that, maybe more. And we'll sell the car, that will be a great buffer in case my jobs aren't enough.*

On an impulse and wanting to save herself the agony of listening to Jake explaining why the contract must be scrapped, she pulled out her phone again and sent him a text, brief and to the point. 'Don't worry about telling me face-to-face, I figured it out. I'll cope.'

Two seconds later he called. 'What *are* you talking about? Would you please explain?'

She blinked hard to hold back the tears that flooded her eyes and tried to sound calm. 'You want to terminate the contract, don't you?'

'Why the hell would I do that? Are you drunk - or did you take something? You sound very strange, Alba.'

'Of course, not - I don't get drunk or take stuff! I

thought probably your wife objects to you being involved with me, even if it's only business, and now she wants you to stop.'

'What wife? I don't have a wife! Where the hell did this come from? You sound really wound-up. I'm going to get in the car and come over, right now! Are you at the warehouse?'

'Who is Samantha Tobin then? Isn't she your wife?'

'Christ, Alba! Who's been feeding you this nonsense? Sam's my brother's wife.'

A sob she couldn't stop burst out. All the pent-up emotions and the depressing feeling that she had fallen in love with someone who would never love her, all her doubts and dark thoughts overwhelmed her.

'I'm sorry!' she said and tried in vain to suppress another sob cracking her voice. 'I saw a photo in the weekend paper at work and it said ...'

'Alba, listen to me!' said Jake firmly. 'Stop! Just listen and please don't cry. I have no wife and no partner of any description, OK? And why I want to explain my plan for Saturday face-to-face is because I want to be absolutely sure you're OK with it - that you won't say yes just because you think you have to. And we need a bit of time because we might have to plan or do a couple of other things to prepare. It has *nothing* to do with ending the contract.'

She wiped her eyes with her free hand while Jake chuckled quietly at the other end. 'Didn't you read it right through? It was only one page, after all, and there's a kind of redundancy clause at the end saying that if I break the contract before the four years are up, I have to pay you the whole amount you would have earned as a lump sum.'

He stopped talking, but before she could say anything he started up again. 'I was embarrassed, if you want to know the truth, you fierce little bully. I feel a bit dicey about what I'm about to suggest about Saturday, but it's definitely not about seducing anyone. All right?'

'I'm sorry,' said Alba contritely and wiped her tear-wet hand on her jeans. 'I jumped to conclusions when I saw that photo in the weekend paper, and then I kind of linked it to the face-to-face thing and got it wrong. Please don't be angry, I was just upset. And it wasn't about the money.'

'I'm not angry, Alba. I could never be angry with you, never - despite that ugly rumour that I growl and scowl like an angry pirate.' She could tell he was smiling. 'I won't jump in the car then - or would you like me to come anyway?'

'God, no, please don't! Go and make some more money or whatever it is you do all day. I'll see you tomorrow.'

After an hour or two her normal calm was nearly back, though she was very aware that she had revealed far too much of her feelings in that phone call. But it might be all right, she thought, trying to comfort herself. Probably someone like Jake had all kinds of women employees who fancied him, so he might not take that sob seriously. And the idea from the night when she had tormented herself by thinking of him, that he probably still thought of her as very young, that was a comfort too, because if he thought of her as kid nearly, then he'd expect her to behave childishly. And added to that were the games she played with him, probably not something anyone else in his employ ever did, also something most people would think was very childish.

Then she laughed silently to herself because the thought of Jake admitting he felt embarrassed was funny, and for the rest of the afternoon she tried to imagine what it was he would ask, interspersed with thoughts about what to make for dessert for dinner that night. Something quick, she thought, not the apple and cinnamon cake her dad loved, it was too late for that and to also make the main course. Maybe baked figs, there were still some ripe ones on the tree in the garden, and she could buy ice cream have with them.

20

Once again Alba got off the bus and walked towards the Scarecrow café in the light drizzle that had persisted for two days. This time Jake was there before her, and she smiled at the sight of him standing there in the rain and hoped he wouldn't bring up her impulsive text message again.

'Jake! You should have gone inside instead of standing around outside. Look at you!'

'Look at you, yourself,' said Jake. 'Wasn't it raining when you left – why aren't you wearing your rain jacket?'

'I threw it away after I sat in that tree. It was covered in sap or whatever that sticky stuff was, it was like glue. It wouldn't come off and I haven't got around to buying a new one.'

He shook his head and held the door open. 'How did the dinner party go? What did you cook?' He sounded casual and calm, and Alba heaved an internal sigh of relief. Maybe they were back to their normal relationship, and he was going to ignore her emotional outburst in that phone call.

'Lamb casserole with root ginger and button mushrooms, baked potatoes and peas with sliced leek mixed in – which is the world's best way to eat peas, and then baked figs with Greek vanilla yoghurt and ice cream.'

'Sounds delicious,' said Jake, as they joined the line at the counter. 'And what else have you been up to since I saw you last?'

Alba turned her head to look in the display cabinet, as if she were contemplating which cake to have and said casually over her shoulder. 'I went out with that American again, but I didn't go to bed with him - OK?'

'Right.' And then after a long silence that turned her senses to high alert he added, 'And is he good kisser?'

She could tell he really wanted to know, there might have been a smidgeon of jealousy hidden in that seemingly teasing question. Still pretending that she was studying the cakes in the cabinet beside her, she said casually, deliberately making it sound as if she was thinking of something else, 'Oh, I wouldn't think so, but I haven't been tempted to let him, he's not a sexy beast, not like …'

'Not like …' then his voice died away, and Alba's heart made a little jump. Had he been about to ask, "like who" and then realised what he had nearly said and managed to stop himself?

'Not like you,' she said, still not looking directly at him and waited with bated breath.

Now the silence between them felt like a physical object, perhaps a large rock, very heavy and probably very difficult to move. Had she made another terrible mistake, gone too far? Maybe *this* time it would be the end of their partnership. Her heart was pounding in her chest making it hard to breathe.

'Me?' his voice held such pleased surprise that she swung around and said, 'Totally! Hasn't anyone told you before?'

His gaze was intense, and she could sense him processing what she had said and imagined the questions he was mentally asking himself. Is she teasing or is it a casual observation or does it mean something? Because suddenly she knew, she could see it in his eyes, his surge of elation and she felt light enough to float to the ceiling after all the uncertainty.

'I knew the moment I met you,' she said and tried to sound light-hearted and casual, but then it was their turn to order and nothing more was said until they sat down at the same table as the first time they met there.

'Alba, I …' said Jake and stopped. Very unlike him, thought Alba, he's usually so decisive and business-like, he must be feeling he's on unstable ground now. I must help him.

'Jake, listen and please don't interrupt,' she said, serious now and intent on getting this right, because another perfect opportunity might never come up - it was now or never. 'I'm going to take a huge risk. I know this is totally wrong, and you're my boss, which I should probably consider before I say this, but I'm going to say it anyway.'

She took a deep breath to steady herself, nearly dizzy with nerves now. 'So, if you want to end our agreement, that's OK. Well, it's not OK - but I would understand why. It's not just that you're a sexy beast, which you are. I love you. And you might think of me as too young to take seriously, even though you know my real age – I know I *look* too young. Or maybe you have something going on with that snooty woman in the red coat? From my side it changes nothing. I still love you. That's why I got so upset yesterday.'

He reached across the table and put his hand on hers, and instantly that feeling of warmth and safety and comfort enveloped her again, just as it had a few weeks ago, but this time there was also a current of desire strong enough to have a colour. It's dark red like wine, she thought, intense and deep. She waited.

'Are you sure?' His voice was hoarse. 'Think of the age gap, I'm old enough to be your father.'

She turned her hand over and curled her fingers around his. 'Teenage dad at seventeen or whatever? Possible, I suppose. Let me tell you about my parents, they're the perfect example. My dad was about forty when he met my mother at a charity function where his band was playing, and she was only twenty, much younger than I am. *Everyone* was against it, on both sides.' She smiled at his serious face, wanted desperately to make him relax, to stop worrying and just accept that she was deadly serious. 'They had all these reasons, that mum was too young, that Steve wasn't Korean, that she *was* Korean, that she was educated, a year away from graduating from university very young, and he was a mechanic, and he was too old – the list of obstacles was endless. But when she turned twenty-one they got married anyway, and they were totally happy, visibly happy, anyone could see it, until the day she died last year.'

And then, because she wanted to make him smile, she added, though she knew it wasn't true, 'Or *have* you got something going on with someone else? What about that rude woman who told me to run off as if I were a naughty five-year-old?'

'God no! She's just someone I know. Her husband left her a few months ago.' He laughed quietly, suddenly he sounded relaxed, back to normal. 'She' been impossible ever since, nobody's safe.'

'She's after *you*,' said Alba darkly and frowned. 'I could tell! The way she looked at you with that ravenous look on her face. She was just about to pounce and knock you to the ground and ravish you right there in the street.'

Jake pushed his chair back and got to his feet. 'Come on - let's go outside for a moment.'

She got up and followed him, and on the way

past the counter he turned to the girl behind the coffee machine. 'Could you put our coffees on the table, please. We'll be back in a minute.'

Outside he took her hand and led her away from the large window before he swung her around to face him, then his hands were framing her face, and she looked up at him with the light rain falling on her skin, adoring the feeling of his hands on her skin and a moment later the feel of his lips on hers. She got up on tiptoes and put her arms around his neck, and the cool rain fell on the back of her hands, but her palms were warm against his skin, and inside her a new sensation spread, something she had never felt before. Desire and total happiness, she thought, this is what it feels like. She ran her fingers through his thick hair and felt him tremble against her and knew this kiss was a seal set on her future. He lifted his head and she let her arms drop, and they stood there looking at each other, silent and dazed. Drops of water fell from Jake's hair onto her forehead as he looked down at her, then his hands once again framed her face, and he ran his thumbs gently over her temples. She closed her eyes and felt his warm breath as he leaned in and kissed her eyelids, and she knew she would remember this moment forever, the tingling sensation when he touched her, the current of desire that ran down her body, the nearly overwhelming feeling of excitement that made her feel as if she were about to cry.

'Sometimes I've wanted to pounce on you and knock you to the ground,' she said with the catch of a sob in her voice, and he held her away from him and studied her face as if he was memorising every expression. Trying to control her voice she added, 'The feeling that I wanted you to touch me has been inside me from that time when you grabbed my wrist.'

She tilted her head and put her cheek against his hand on her shoulder. He lifted his other hand and ran a finger over her rain-wet cheek and down the side of her neck and she shivered.

Jake let his hands drop, touched the tip of her nose and smiled. 'You're getting too wet, you'll get cold – I need to get you out of the rain.'

They stepped apart, smiled at each other and went inside, both of them very wet now. She was watching us, thought Alba, as she took in the smile on the face of the girl at the coffee machine. That look - as if we're sharing a secret. She smiled back as they passed.

21

Once they were sitting down again Alba noted how calm they both were now, as if nothing particularly exciting had happened. She liked that they were alike in so many strange little ways, like this ability to switch moods and adopt a calm facade.

'But listen - there's something I don't understand,' she said and picked up her coffee cup which was cooling rapidly. 'What's all this secrecy about? I mean the dinner tomorrow night. What is it you want me to do? Is it another business deal you're not sure of?'

'Kind of. There's a guy called John Williams, who's been after getting on the board at MoreIT for a while now, very keen, waiting for someone to resign or be voted out. I think he knows quite a lot about both IT and business. He's making a full-time career out of being on the boards of successful companies. And now he's found out that one board member is resigning at the AGM because of ill-health – well, let's be honest, she's dying. He might be useful on the board, but I don't think I want him there.'

Alba failed to see what the connection was; it seemed pretty straight forward. 'Why are you suspicious – isn't he a good fit? Do you know something bad about him?'

'I've heard he likes to wield influence generally, or you could call it throwing his weight around. A couple of years ago he made a statement in an interview about another company where he was taking a seat on the board. He said he feels those who started and built a company should step back from what he called too much personal involvement once a company was listed on the stock exchange. His opinion is that the founder could hold innovative development back by influencing board members. I think John would be divisive and potentially waste a lot of time at board meetings. He might try to get the board to vote for changing the company constitution, to side-line me out of some of my roles.'

Alba stared out the window while she tried to work out what this might mean. After a few moments while Jake watched her without saying anything, she turned back to him. 'I thought the company constitution was decided when a company was formed and only the company directors, not those on the board, could change it. How could the board force a change? Or do you think he'd just be a pain and argue about things for the sake of it?'

Jake smiled and she could feel how pleased he was with her reaction. 'That's my girl! Exactly the right questions to ask. But all members of the board of directors are listed as directors of the company with the Companies Office. And they *can* change the constitution.' He frowned. 'I have a very close to majority shareholding, but I regret now that I only kept forty-five percent of the shareholding when I went public. if I had an outright majority I could vote against John getting on the board at the Annual General Meeting.'

'But wouldn't he have to get lots of shareholders on his side?' asked Alba after thinking for a few moments. 'If he gets together more shareholders so that group have more than your forty-five percent, then they could get him made a director, couldn't they?'

'That's right, but he'd have to get practically everyone either on his side, or he'd have to buy loads of shares. And I don't' want him on the board being a nuisance, disrupting board meetings with power plays and silly stuff, which to date we've never had. We've always had a very cooperative board with no egos making themselves obnoxious. And I'd like to keep it that way, so this is where my plan comes in.'

There was that slight uneasiness again, very slight, but Alba could hear it as a layer of worry under the surface of his voice.

'Jake, please tell me what this is about! I know you're hesitating about something and it's so unlike you.'

'Let's have lunch now,' said Jake instead of explaining. 'We can go to the sushi place again, or somewhere else, and I'll tell you the details. This place is too noisy now and the tables are so close together.'

'Anywhere they don't have uni-sex toilets. You choose this time.'

On the way to the Japanese restaurant Jake unexpectedly asked, 'Will you let me order for both of us?'

'OK,' said Alba. 'I trust you, so yes, you can order for both of us. Is it something special?'

'It's okonomiyaki – have you had it?'

'Never even heard of it.' Alba laughed under her breath. 'But if there was ever a day to try okono-what's-it, today is obviously the right day.' She saw his sideways glance out of the corner of her eye and smiled. 'It's true, I don't know what it is, but I'm all for new things happening today. You could probably make me do anything.'

'Don't tempt me!'

'Now, do you think you can listen without interrupting me, so I can tell you what I'd like us to do tomorrow?' said Jake when he had ordered and asked the waiter not to serve their meal for at least half an hour. 'I need the time to get this right to avoid misunderstandings, but it's going to be easier now after the little episode outside Scarecrow. Would you like a glass of wine?'

'Am I going to need it? Like something to lessen the shock and outrage?'

'You might need it and if you don't, we'll call it a celebration.'

When their glasses of wine had arrived, Jake launched into his plan. 'This dinner tomorrow night is with two couples, John and his wife, whose name I've forgotten and a couple I invited because they're very good friends of mine and they'll act like a buffer zone and make it seem less about business and more like a genuine social event. And they'll also help with the plan. Yes?'

Alba's hand had shot up in the air, as if she was back at school. 'Do those people already know each other? And who set up the dinner?'

'You're on to it again, you amazing girl. I set up the dinner date when I met John at an event a couple of weeks ago and he said we must get together for a meal sometime before the annual general meeting. He's been working on softening me up for a while to get me to back him, so I organised this dinner myself because I wanted to be able to decide who was present. So, if you agree, my plan is to introduce you as my fiancée and …'

Up went her hand again. 'Is this a real engagement or just pretend?'

'Would you like it to be real?'

She knew he wasn't joking, just how serious he was came across like a forceful emotion that made her smile inside. 'Yes please!'

'OK, then it's a real engagement. What a crazy way to propose!' He laughed. 'This is going much better than I thought it would. I hadn't counted on your love declaration in the café, and I thought you might protest or refuse, or walk out on me or something.'

'Listen, Jake,' said Alba using her adult voice. 'And this is for real and no exaggeration. I'll refuse you *nothing*, apart from rough sex, of course, but nothing else ever. I want you to be happy. It makes me happy just thinking of you being happy.'

He put his hand on hers again and she said quickly, before he could comment, 'Please let's continue talking about the dinner and not get emotional, or I might start to cry right here in public and if I start I might not be able to stop. I'm so happy I could burst, and I can feel tears just waiting to run down my face. And I won't interrupt again. I really want to know what you've planned.'

The way he looked at her told her everything she most wanted to know, and she felt instantly calmer, enveloped in his warm strength. Just having him look at me like that is like a hug, she thought, just thinking of his hands on my skin makes me tremble, but I must hold it in and concentrate, this is important.

'I'll brief my friends tonight,' said Jake, 'so they

understand what I want them to say and do tomorrow. I want to introduce you to John and his wife as my fiancée, as I said, which will be reinforced by my friends, Pete and Monica, who will greet you as a friend, as if they've met you lots of times. And don't look at me like that – they'll do what I ask, they trust me. And at some stage during the dinner, I'll manage to casually mention that you're a shareholder now – that you've bought shares in MoreIT. And I'll say that I'm going to propose you as the replacement director at the AGM.'

'But …' said Alba, then she clapped her hand over her mouth. 'Oh, sorry, I interrupted.'

'Go ahead, I wasn't serious - what were you going to say?'

'But I haven't bought any shares - I don't have the money to do it.'

'You have bought shares. Or rather your trust has invested in More IT shares.'

Alba stared at him and wondered if she had lost her mind. She could make no sense of what he just said and now a fast-moving surge of worry came across the table in a huge wave and invaded her mind and made her flinch. This was what had made him so hesitant, but what did it mean?

She opened her mouth to speak, but he held his hand up, palm out. 'Hang on, let me tell you – and hear me out, right to the end before you react. I've gone way too far probably, but if I have, then you still benefit.' He drank some of his wine and looked straight into her eyes. 'I have set up the Alba Asher Trust. I did it a week ago and the trust has bought shares from small shareholders since then, quite a few. Nearly enough to give your trust and myself an unbeatable combined majority for voting at the AGM. I'll mention the trust at the dinner in a reply to a question Pete will ask and then say I'm proposing you as the new board member. Possibly the other way around, but the main thing is that you'll be on the board.'

Alba looked hard at him. 'And where did that trust get its money from? And what's the aim of the trust – don't trusts have to have a specific aim?'

'I set it up for the benefit of your children's and you – primarily for education, but also other needs, very wide. The money came from me, but once it was in the trust's account I can't take it back.'

Alba giggled, despite how confused she still felt. 'So technically I could have triplets with the mailman, and you'd be paying for their education via the profits the trust makes from dividends? Are you crazy? It's like giving heaps of money away.'

'If you don't want to be on the board of directors you'll still have the trust – the letters to you and Steve from my lawyers about the formalities of both of you becoming trustees are in the mail right now. And if you hadn't made the love declaration you would still have had the trust and the benefits it brings. Nothing can change that.'

She sat silently staring at him while her brain slotted these facts into two scenarios, one where she never told him she loved him, and the one they were in now, and knew he was the most unbelievable person she had ever met.

'And now for the best bit,' said Jake. 'I want you to arrive with me, dressed up and looking expensive and best of all, a bit severe, serious. No effusive sweetness from you, just a friendly greeting to Pete and Monica, and affection towards me, of course. But be stand-offish in a subtle way with John and his wife, as if maybe I've warned you about something. As if I've told you something about him and you don't totally trust him. Could you do that, do you think?'

The waiter arrived just then with plates and a large platter with something flat and flaky on it and put it in the middle of the table. Alba tried to figure out what it was, some kind of Japanese pizza type thing? Or a pancake? She voiced these options and Jake smiled. 'Pancake more than pizza. It's filled with savoury things, usually cabbage and pork, and it's delicious. I hope you're not a vegetarian.'

'No, I'm an omnivore. What are those flakes on top? I've never seen anything like it before.'

He picked up the menu, studied it for a moment and said, 'Fish flakes and dried seaweed, and underneath that a savoury sauce of some kind, not soy I don't think, something else. Try a piece! I've only had it once or twice, and you don't find it everywhere, but I noticed it on the menu last time we were here.'

'Oh God, it's wonderful!' said Alba after one

mouthful. 'Absolutely wonderful! But to go back to your plan. It sounds OK, and I think I can do the acting, but I have to confess I don't own a single expensive looking thing. I'll have to do some quick shopping, but I don't know what you would regard as expensive and severe looking. To be quite honest, I have no idea at all. Classy and severe has never been my thing. I shop in chain stores and malls and buy pretty or practical things.'

'We'll go shopping after lunch,' said Jake calmly and ate some okonomiyaki. 'That's why I said we might need some extra time. I'll text Sam, she's a fabulous dresser and she'll tell us where to go. And now I'll fill you in on Pete and Monica's children and a few other things, so you can interact in a natural way with them tomorrow.'

Armed with a text message listing shopping suggestions from Samantha they set out on the most exciting shopping expedition Alba had ever made.

'Let's take a taxi,' said Jake and made Alba laugh. 'Taxi? Why don't we just run? Or we can walk if you prefer.'

'Well, seeing the rain has nearly stopped, let's walk then. Do you ever shop in the city?'

'No, and I've never been on a real shopping expedition either,' she confessed as they walked away from the restaurant. 'Mostly I just go somewhere with a friend, some place with reasonable prices and pretty things, and we wander around and look at things. I've never bought anything even remotely classy because I've never needed anything like that. I did buy a nice black dress for mum's funeral, it's pretty, but it's not classy, I don't think. My friend Linley would know, but I've never really paid much attention to clothes. You'll have to help me.'

22

Two hours later, after first stopping at a sports shop to buy a rain jacket for Alba, she was in a fourth fitting rom, wearing a sleeveless black dress with a neckline the shop assistant called a boat neck. When she had helped Alba do up the zip at the back, she studied her in the mirror and murmured, 'You look so exotic in that dress.'

It made Alba laugh. 'Pure Onehunga bred, nothing exotic about me apart from being half Korean.'

The woman smiled. 'Doesn't matter where you live,' she said. 'It's that gorgeous mix, you *look* exotic. I thought you must be half something and half something else when you first came in – a mix always comes out best, I think. The designer calls this dress Moon River.'

'That's a song my mother used to sing! From some old movie.'

'From Breakfast at Tiffany's with Audrey

Hepburn,' said the assistant. 'I haven't seen it, but I know the tune of course. On the posters for the film, she wears a dress just like this but without the slot.'

'Stunning!' said Jake when she pulled the curtain back to show him. 'My God, you look like a million dollars – it's perfect.'

'Not far off a million dollars - the price tag made my eyes water,' said Alba. 'But there's a stack of dresses in there I haven't even tried on yet, I just started with this one because I loved the look of it, kind of severe and minimal.'

'No, this one's perfect, very classy, don't bother with the others. I like that letterbox slot. Very intriguing ...'

His eyes met hers and Alba felt her skin tingle, as if her body was anticipating the feel of his hands on her skin, and a blush rose up her face.

The immaculate and slightly intimidating woman who had assisted Alba, watched this unspoken exchange without betraying what she was thinking, held back the curtain to the fitting room and said, 'Now we need to have a little chat, you and I.'

She gave Jake a look that nearly made Alba laugh out loud. He's been dismissed with a glance, she thought, how funny, I bet that doesn't happen very often.

'You must have a different bra to wear with that dress,' said the assistant in a low voice once she had pulled the curtain across behind them. 'The whole point of what your partner called the letterbox slot is this.'

She put her hands on Alba's shoulder and turned her towards the mirror, then both her hands came around from behind and one hand stretched the fabric of the dress down, then the other hand pushed Alba's little breasts up.

'See what I mean? That slot is a teaser, a temptation. Like an understated promise. It's meant to hint at what a more revealing dress might flaunt and make completely obvious. So, you need a push-up bra.'

'I've never had one of those,' said Alba. 'I've never needed one.'

While the assistant kept her hands on her, Alba studied her reflection and saw what she meant. The push-up bra would raise her breasts, and the upper curve would show in the horizontal slot. Far more subtle than a low-cut neckline, and somehow more enticing.

'I see what you mean,' she said slowly. 'It's the epitome of less is more, isn't it?'

The woman laughed and dropped her hands. 'Exactly! But I've just had an idea, I think we can do it without a new bra, just wait here a moment.'

Sellotape, wondered Alba, or gaffer tape? Ouch! Does she keep a roll in the back room? But what the assistant handed her were two skin-coloured silicone half cups with rounded extensions, like rabbit ears or fingers.

'These will adhere to you skin, believe it or not,'

she said. 'You position them by holding each breast up and then put them in place. Place that rabbit ears just under the bottom curve of your breast and then fit the cup upward. It works really well. No straps and very comfortable. I'll give you these for free.' She smiled. 'I've rarely had such a gorgeous girl to find the perfect dress for. You're very lucky! Mostly the women who have the money to shop here are a bit older or not *quite* as perfect as you are. It's been a pleasure.'

When they left the shop with a shiny black carrier bag with plaited cord handles, Jake suddenly stopped. 'Shoes – do we need to get black shoes?'

'Oh heavens, I don't wear high heels very often, but I think I must with this dress. I'll get some tomorrow. No, don't say we'll buy them now, I think you've spent more than enough money on me.'

This time the frown didn't appear at the idea that she would pay for herself, and Alba smiled inside. For some reason what she had told him in the café, what he had referred to as her love declaration, had changed things in more than one respect. She couldn't for the life of her imagine why, but it had, and she would work it out over time. Or why don't I just ask him, she thought and smiled at the thought of how many inappropriate and nearly rude questions and accusations she had already fired at him without the least hesitation.

They sat in a bistro for half an hour discussing the details of the dinner the next day, then Jake bundled Alba into a taxi despite her protests and paid up-front for the fare to Onehunga. He cupped her cheek in his hand and smiled, and she leaned into his palm for a moment, but neither of them made any move to kiss or hug, and Alba smiled again.

We're different from other people, she thought, as the car filtered out into the heavy Friday afternoon traffic. We don't need to say things, we know anyway. Nothing shows on his face, but I can feel it. And minimal displays of public affection, that's us, apart from kissing like maniacs on the pavement outside the café, of course. He looks at me and my skin reacts, I tease him, and I know he's having fun, and I can feel how much he wants me. That smouldering look in the shop! My God, I hope he doesn't do that in public too often, it nearly set me on fire.

All the way to Onehunga Alba debated with herself about what she should tell Steve about her trip into town and all that had happened. Thinking back over her relationship with Jake she realised that it might seem impossible to someone else, who had not heard their style of teasing, not felt his secret amusement, not witnessed his concern when he held her close and told her she was safe. Even thinking of how he had held her then made her feel happy. His arms around her back, the feel of his body, the way his voice made the trauma from the incident on the bus recede into the background.

It will seem mad, she thought and looked unseeingly out the taxi window. Those things were like little signals, little hints, but only he and I know that and understand the subtext. The engagement will seem like too abrupt a change, too surprising and perhaps also too unequal to take seriously. She remembered her dad telling her of all the differences between her mother and him, the things people had objected to, and thought he would probably understand. Some of those concerns applied to her and Jake, too, but with the added complication of his wealth. Would people make simplistic assumptions about what motivated her? When the taxi stopped outside her house, she still hadn't made up her mind about what to tell her father or when.

'There you are!' he said when she walked in. 'I looked in the fridge and saw there's enough of last night's dinner for us to have tonight. I'm just about to put it in the oven to heat. And look at that fancy bag – did you leave work early to go shopping?'

'It's a very long story, dad. I'll tell you over dinner. You're only going to believe it if I tell it right and you don't distract me. Let's leave it for now and I'll go and clean my teeth – I had a super Japanese lunch and a glass of wine.'

She walked down the hallway to her room and pictured him standing there staring after her, half puzzled, half amused. At least I won't have to draw a series of sketches to explain things this time, she said to herself as she cleaned her teeth and studied her face in the bathroom mirror. He might not believe me, or he might think Jake was joking and I've taken it seriously or something, but I can deal with that.

The shiny black bag lay unopened on her bed and when she touched it she felt nearly overwhelmed. Before she put the dress on a hanger in her wardrobe she held it up in front of her and studied herself in the long mirror on the back of her door. In her mind she pictured the scene when she came out of the fitting room, the way he looked at her and the current of warmth and desire that flowed from him, the strong emotions that felt as if his hands touched her. Never before had anyone had such a strong connection that a glance felt like a physical touch, she thought. She remembered the way he had kept an eye on her when they walked to that Japanese restaurant that first time, and she had felt his sideways glances as light touches on her shoulder. Already at that time he was looking after me, she thought, caring about me and I felt his feelings as a touch. She smiled as she closed her bedroom door behind her and went to join Steve.

23

Steve was watching the news when Alba returned from her room, so she busied herself with setting the table and checking the oven, so by the time she joined her father in front of the TV he seemed to have forgotten about the fancy bag. Rather than remind him she took the opportunity to consider how to start her story, slightly doubtful about what approach would work best.

'What's in that fancy bag?' asked Steve when they were sitting down to dinner. 'And how come you had Japanese food with wine for lunch? You didn't go out with that American guy again, did you?'

'No, I was with Jake,' said Alba and impulsively abandoned her plan to tell him a long and detailed story to make the engagement seem believable. 'And he proposed, and I said "yes, please" and then we went shopping.'

There was silence while Steve finished chewing a mouthful of lamb casserole and Alba sat unmoving with every nerve jangling, her fork suspended over her plate, until he swallowed and said calmly, 'Great!' and reached for his glass of beer.

She burst out laughing and put her fork down. 'That's *all*? Great? No questions, no objections, no comments?'

'Well, it is great, isn't it?' said her father reasonably. 'I like the guy, he's very honest and upfront and not at all up himself about what he's achieved. We got to know each other quite fast that morning when we thought you were lost, you know. We were both absolutely terrified that something awful had happened to you, I could see how worried he was, though he didn't say it. I'd called him late the night before when you didn't come home, and he said right away he'd come over first thing. And he did, he was here just before dawn. I had already notified the police the night before, and they confirmed your car was in the carpark, so we both knew something awful must have happened.'

'What did you talk about?'

'Oh, all kinds of things,' said Steve casually, and she could tell he was having fun now. 'Mostly about someone he called his favourite little bully. He told me some things you and he had talked about, and how you can read him like a book – that's how he put it himself. He said you're the only person who's ever been able to do that, and how clever you are and funny and cheeky. He didn't say anything really personal, but I'm not as green as I'm cabbage looking. I had no problem seeing where this was going – provided you felt the same way of course.'

Alba was astounded to hear that Jake had discussed her in those terms with her dad; not at all what she had expected, and she felt herself blushing at the thought of those two maybe discussing her in more detail than her father was letting on.

'And what did you say when he told you I was a little bully? Did you defend me?'

'No, I told him your mother was exactly the same, and you're so like her it reminds me of her every day.'

Alba decided it was time to change the subject before he had them both in tears. 'I'll tell you what he wants me to do tomorrow night, just an outline, and then I'll tell you how it turned out later on, after the event. I've got to buy a pair of black high heels tomorrow and a little bag to go with my new dress, and then Jake's coming to pick me up at six, so you'll see the dress we bought today. No – correction - *we* didn't buy it, he did. It cost approximately the same as the national debt, so it was way out of my league.'

When she had finished the outline of Jake's plan for the dinner her father looked confused. 'But why? What's the point? It's not going to change anything in particular, is it? I just don't get it - such an elaborate thing to set up and no particular result that I can see. And are you really going to be on the board? It sounds mad. You don't know enough about big business.'

How could she explain it? To her it was very clear now, a strategy to draw a line of immutable intent in the sand, to make sure things went the way Jake wanted them to go without fuss and conflict.

'There are a couple of things that Jake wants to achieve,' she said after thinking for a moment. 'Let's have drink, I mean a wine we both like, not you with a beer and me drinking a wine I like. You're not going to work tomorrow, so it doesn't matter. You get the ice cream out and I'll open a bottle of that wine that mum kept for when she made a special dinner, that red you like. There are still a couple of bottles in the pantry.'

They sat in the living room and Alba turned her chair at right angles to her father's so they could look at each other instead of facing the TV, the way they usually sat.

'Here goes then. There's a guy called John Williams, who's business savvy and on some company boards already, and now he's very keen to be on MoreIT's board, but Jake has reservations. Apparently John is a bit of an ego type person, likes to wield power, as Jake calls it. He might turn out to be trouble on the board, and they've never had anyone troublesome before, it seems to have been a hand-picked bunch of people who've been able to function in harmony for years, but one of them is resigning because she's seriously ill. And Jake's way to make sure John knows he's not going to have Jake's support, much less be proposed by him for the board, is to use me as the chess piece that knocks John off the board – pun intended.'

Steve looked thoughtful and continued slowly eating ice cream while Alba waited for the questions she knew would be coming, and then she remembered she had left out one of the key bits of information.

'Oh yes, and also this – at the moment, Jake's busy buying more shares from small shareholders in my name, nothing to do with him, so I'll actually own them.'

She paused for a moment with a frown, wondering if telling him about the trust now would create a need for long explanations or not but decided he had to know.

'He has set up a trust in my name with me as the beneficiary, and the trust is buying the shares. Two things will come from this - John will realise there's little point in trying to link himself up with enough small shareholders and start something Jake calls a bloc move at the AGM in May because by then the trust will have enough shares for it – which means me - and Jake together to have a majority. And John won't be able to form an effective voting bloc, that's a bloc without the "k", which I hadn't come across before. He's sure to find some shareholder to nominate him for the board, but he won't get enough votes.'

'Bloody heck,' exclaimed Steve and sat up

straighter. 'You mean Jake's doing all this in your name and you'll own shares, or that trust will, and you'll really sit on the board and all that? What if you take off and leave him? Doesn't that worry him? You could cause mayhem for him – just take off and you'd still have that trust, wouldn't you?'

'I never thought of that,' said Alba slowly. 'We didn't talk about that angle at all. It just didn't occur to either of us. I don't think I could leave him, not ever. It's like there's a bond, dad, and quite often we just know things without talking about them. It's really hard to describe, but I knew it from the start, right from when I talked to him on the phone the first time, when I told him about the unconditional no, and he chuckled. I thought it was only me at first, I mean who felt like that, but it was the same for him - he just didn't do anything or say anything because he was sure I thought he was way too old.'

'Explain what you mean by a bond,' said Steve. 'Like an emotional link, a connection? Like what Mary and I had? Something you feel sure can't be broken, that you both know is so strong that it will be forever?'

'Exactly like that,' said Alba, and although she and Jake had not discussed it, only mentioned it briefly, but she knew it was true. 'It's not lust or infatuation or anything simplistic or short-lived like that. It sounds mad when I say it, but I know how strong it is - it will last.'

At bedtime, when Alba picked up her phone for the first time since she got home, there was a message from Jake. Understated as usual it read, *Might be good to bring an overnight bag? We could be late. J*

And Alba replied in the same vein, smiling to herself as she did so. *OK, will do. Axx*

Just before she fell asleep she thought of what she had said to Steve and how that bond she had tried to describe was so real in her mind. It's like an open channel of unspoken feelings and comfort and desire, she thought, like a constant flow between us. We are so lucky!

24

When Alba texted Linley early on Saturday morning and asked if she would like to come on a shopping trip to get shoes and a bag for a special occasion, and said she wanted to go to the Outlet Mall, Linley called straight back.

'Not there, but I know just where to go,' she said enthusiastically. 'You know those gorgeous shoes I bought for Zac's brother's wedding? The silvery ones you admired when I showed you and said they looked like shoes for an angel to wear? I got them at Overland, they have nice shoes and bags too, but maybe not terribly many bags and it's not a super expensive place, so you won't pay several hundred dollars. And if we don't see anything you like there, I have a mental list of other shops to try. Or we could go into town and have a look there.'

Alba smiled. 'You're the only person I know who

buys quality stuff – so let's start at Overland. I'll pick you up at ten.'

'I'm going out early,' said Alba to her dad when they were making breakfast. 'I'm picking Linley up and we're going to find some shoes I can wear with the national debt dress tonight, and a bag. I refused to have Jake pay for everything like he thought he should.'

It was easy to find the right shoes, but the bag was a different matter. 'No!' said Alba decisively when Linley suggested a little shoulder bag on a gold chain. 'It's got to be some kind of little flat bag I can carry in my hand. You haven't seen the dress, but it's seriously classy and super minimal. It fits like a glove, no sleeves, and a boat neck, which I'd never heard of before, but I'm sure you know what it means. And it's got a horizonal slit across the front, just at the top of my boobs. It's extremely elegant and it cost a bomb. We'll have to go somewhere else for the bag.'

'If you don't tell me who this guy is who paid for the dress – and *soon* - I'll throw myself on the floor and scream,' said Linley, who had held back her questions though she was clearly bursting with curiosity. She paused for a moment. 'But seriously, what you mean is a clutch bag,' 'I think we'll have to go into town. Or maybe to Sylvia Park, to that Korean shop full of faux stuff – they have fabulous things that look as if they cost a fortune.'

'And what do they really cost?' Alba considered her bank account, the shoes she had just paid for and the automatic transfer to the mortgage account that would go out on Monday. 'I refuse to spend more than fifty dollars on a bag however classy the dress is. We'll have to find a bag that's just pretend classy.'

As they headed towards the Sylvia Park mall Linley, confident that they would find something Alba liked, continued talking about clutch bags she had seen there and in the city. But Alba got progressively more dejected at the prospect of appearing as the sophisticated and elegant fiancée for Jake to show off that evening.

'You know what?' she said despondently when she had parked the car. 'I'm not sure I'll be able to carry this off. Shoes, dress, bag, yeah, fine. But my head, my face! Look at me - I have this thick straight black hair that I never do anything with apart from sometimes put it up in a topknot, and I never use make-up. I'm going to look ridiculous with all this new gear, like my head's been transplanted onto someone else's body.'

'You're being silly,' said Linley bracingly. 'You're just having last minute nerves because it's all so new to you. Let's find a place to have lunch so we can make a plan.'

She slid a sideways look at Alba. 'And don't look like that, it's not like you. You just suddenly got scared. Not that you've told me much about this guy and the dinner, but I'll help you get your head and face to match your new clothes, so he's satisfied with your appearance. Glamour is what we want, it will make you feel confident.'

They had a quick, simple lunch and Linley proved as good as her word, the way she had many times when calm was needed ever since Alba was five and Linley was ten and they walked to school together. Alba sat quietly eating her ham sandwich and listened to her friend putting in place a step-by-step plan for the afternoon.

'First we find the bag, then we go to MAC and buy some make-up for you, then we go back to my place, and I'll do your face and hair. Can you get into that dress without ruining your hair if I put it up?'

'It's got a zip right down to my bum at the back,' said Alba. 'If it didn't, you couldn't get into it – it's that tight. It's even got a little thing like a string with a hook on the end that you can hook into the zipper thing, so you can pull it up yourself if you don't have anyone to help you.'

'Can't wait to see it,' said Linley, drank the last of her coffee and put the cup down with a bang. 'Let's get going! And promise to take a photo tonight – get your dad to do it before you go out. I've got to see the full effect.'

They were walking away from the café when Alba had a sudden thought. 'What's make-up from that MAC place going to cost? Isn't that an expensive place? I can't afford to spend too much –

remember I told you how we're paying off the mortgage really fast?'

'We must be psychic! I was just thinking that I'll give you the make-up as an early birthday present,' said Linley, and Alba thought she had just made that up, but it was a lovely present. 'I never quite know what to get you, and this little expedition has been such fun, like a new venture for you and me. We've never done this, have we? You're not usually into clothes and stuff that I love – and I know what I'm doing.'

'We don't want blatant or uber glamourous,' said Linley two hours later when she put Alba into a reclining armchair in her living room and tipped it right back, much to Zac's amusement.

'Go away, Zac!' she ordered. 'This is serious, and I need to concentrate. I've never done someone else's make-up before, and I need to get it right. You can come and look when it's finished.'

She refused to let Alba look in a mirror when she had finished the make-up, just made her pull her T-shirt off and lent her a shirt. 'You've got to be able to get out of it without ruining your hair,' she explained. 'I'm going to do something really special. I've just had a fabulous idea, a thing I saw in a magazine, but I have to work out how to get it to work. This is such fun!'

Half an hour later Alba stared mesmerised into their bathroom mirror and noticed that Zac had followed them and was standing in the doorway with an awestruck look on his face.

'Oh my God!' was all Alba could say, overcome by the transformation. It was not only the lovely make-up, but the topknot that was made up of several thick swirls of hair that interlocked tightly and had two shiny, black sticks crossing through it, so they stuck up in a V-shape.

'You've made me beautiful! And what are those things in my hair? Where did you get them?'

'Oh, they're a pair of Japanese lacquered chopsticks from a set we were given as a wedding present. They're so beautiful with that gold pattern running down them. They make you look like you're out of a fairy tale, or perhaps a manga cartoon.' She laughed. 'They'll be great for self-defence too, they've got very pointy ends, which are facing down for safety reasons. Bet you could probably stab someone through the heart with them if you had to.'

'I'll be like a piece of sushi when I get into that tight black dress!' Alba laughed and noticed Zac's eyes still on her reflection and realised that Linley had truly turned her into someone else.

'But a very elegant piece of sushi. God, you look so lovely! I can't wait to hear what that guy says when he sees you,' said Linley and gave Alba a teasing glance. 'And when are you going to tell me who he is and what he does, and all that? It's not like you to be so secretive. I was sure it would slip out while we were shopping or having lunch.'

'I've told you his name is Jacob, and he's asked me to do this as a favour, just to see if I can help him. It's a business thing, but he needs me to put on an act at this dinner tonight,' said Alba, who hadn't told Linley any more than she had to and made no mention of the engagement. She still felt overwhelmed by the rapid progression of what she had thought for so long was her private infatuation and wasn't ready to share it quite yet.

'I helped him once before and he was pleased about that, but I don't know how well the acting tonight is going work. He's using me as a tool, an expensive tool if you think of what he's spent on me, but I've got to look the part. And I'll get a wonderful meal and lovely wine in some fancy restaurant, so I'm not complaining. Plus, the amazing sushi dress!'

25

When Alba finally got home at quarter past five, Steve was in the vegetable garden, so she called out to him through the open back door and said she must change right away and disappeared into her room. The first thing she did was stare mesmerised at her face in the mirror again, just as she had at Linley's place. She thought of how Zac had looked at her, as if he had never seen her before, and she felt the same way herself. From someone who had never bothered with make-up apart from lipstick sometimes, she had been transformed into an exotic creature; someone who combined style and glamour with something a little like severity, and though she had not mentioned that word to Linley, it was what she had achieved with the elaborate topknot and the chopsticks. The image she presented would be perfect for her role. She told herself to remember when looking straight at John, that she mustn't smile too widely, just a tiny smile with a serious look behind it, perhaps a thoughtful look. Standing back from the mirror she tried it and decided thoughtful would work. It was a good mix, politely friendly with an overlay of reserve.

After putting a change of clothes and her trainers into the little overnight bag she was taking to Jake's she tried to think what else she might need, added the gorgeous makeup bag Linley had packed her new things into, and zipped the bag up. A moment later she opened it again and added underwear, socks and her toothbrush and hoped she hadn't left out anything vital, but her stress levels were sky high now, and she found it hard to concentrate. The process of putting the uplifter cups on was easier than she had expected, but pulling the zip up at the back of the dress tested her patience. The last thing she wanted was to have to ask Steve for help because somehow the idea that he and Jake must see her at the same time had taken on a level of importance in her mind, which she couldn't quite understand, so she struggled on until she managed.

At five to six she heard a car on the drive and Steve's footsteps as he walked down the hall to open the front door, then his and Jake's voices, though she couldn't hear what they were saying. She stood with her hand on the doorhandle and counted to ten to give them enough time to go into the living room, which she felt certain would be where her father had taken Jake, then she opened the door. For some unaccountable reason she was suddenly nervous to show herself all done up to look like somebody else, so tense she was nearly trembling. She walked slowly down the hallway with her little square clutch bag covered in mother-of-pearl tiles in her hand, her body taut with a mixture of nerves and excitement.

'Holy hell, darling!' said Steve when she came into the living room, his eyes wide. Jake just stared for a moment and then he smiled. 'Stunning!' he said and his look sweeping over her nearly scorched her skin, then suddenly she was calm again. There was a moment of silence while the men continued to look at her, and she thought, yes! she could do this, and then Steve broke the spell. 'What an incredible dress - and the hair! I don't know who you are tonight, but it's not my little Alba.'

Then he chuckled and turned to Jake with a look of someone who's just discovered something important. 'Hey, you two have forgotten something, I think! Just wait here, I'll be back in a moment.'

He left them standing silently looking at each other; Jake's eyes still roving over her, and Alba, now calm, looking back at him with every inch of her body tingling. When Steve returned and Alba saw the little, red leather box in his hand she knew instantly what they had forgotten. Inside the box was her mother's diamond engagement ring, the one she had worn on a chain around her neck until she graduated at twenty-one and they got married.

'I'm giving you Mary's engagement ring. If

you're going to be convincingly engaged in front of that guy tonight she's got to have a ring,' he said and laughed when Alba put her hand out for the box. Holding it high out of her reach he said, 'No, no, no - you're not getting engaged to *me*, Miss Bossy. I'm giving it to Jake, so he can give it to you.'

And that's what they did. Steve put the ring on the palm of Jake's hand, and he put it on Alba's finger and her eyes filled with tears. 'It feels as if mum is here with us,' she said and took her father's hand. 'Thank you, dad! I won't hug you, or I might poke one of your eyes out.'

Before they left Steve took a photo of them together, then Alba did hug him, very carefully tilting her head back to keep the chopsticks out of the way, picked up her little overnight bag and said casually, 'See you tomorrow, dad.'

Outside in the cool of the early evening Jake held the car door open for her before he got into the driver's seat and reversed out of the driveway.

'You look so fantastic I can't find words,' he said and reached across to touch her hand. 'Where's my fierce little bully girl? You'll totally bowl everyone over tonight. I knew you'd be convincing, but this is another level – jaw-dropping.'

'It's not really me - it's all thanks to Linley,' said Alba. 'She kind of invented a different me. She's my best friend, and she did my face and my hair because I wouldn't have a clue how to apply this kind of make-up. But we bought lots, so I can teach myself in case I need to do it again - or more likely, she'll teach me.' She grinned at the memory of their foray into MAC and how Linley had walked around picking up one item after another without hesitation. 'She even made me buy a bottle of special stuff to get it off my face. She said soap and water wouldn't do it properly.'

Five minutes later Jake abruptly pulled into a bus stop and turned in his seat. 'I love you,' he said, and his eyes were serious. 'I only realised later that I didn't say it yesterday, but I've loved you from the first time I met you. I was fascinated when you explained the unconditional no in our first phone call, but when you started in on the campaign of cheeky comments and telling me off, I was lost.'

She stared into his eyes in the early evening golden light that made his hair more russet than chestnut and said slowly, 'You feel that thing too, don't you? That channel between us, so we know what sits behind what we actually say? I thought I could feel it was a two-way thing early on, and then I thought I was probably fooling myself because I was ...' Her voice tapered off while she continued to look into his eyes.

'What were you? Tell me what you're thinking.'

She hesitated only a moment. 'I was falling in love with you so fast and so deeply – it felt unreal, as if it couldn't possibly turn into anything.'

'I know, me too.' He ran his fingers over her cheek and down her neck and just like the previous time he did it, electricity fizzed across her skin. 'Let's go now. I'll tell you a bit more about what Pete and Monica have worked out, things to make it seem like a long-standing connection.' He lifted her hand, kissed her knuckles, and pulled out on the street again.

Alba had imagined that they would go straight to the restaurant and leave her overnight bag in the car, but Jake drove to an apartment block in the Wynyard Quarter and parked in an underground garage.

'Right,' he said. 'This is where I live, and hopefully where we will live, if you like it. So, let's go up and leave your overnight bag, and then we'll take a taxi to the restaurant.'

'Where is it we're going for dinner?' asked Alba as they took the lift to level five.

'The Grove. It's very good, I hope you'll enjoy it.'

'What are you staring at, Boss-man? Is something wrong with my make-up – did Linley put on too much?'

'Not at all, it's perfect. I'm just looking at your mouth.'

'Why? Because it talks too much?'

'I love your mouth, it's delicious. And I was wondering if we can wipe the lipstick off, so I can kiss you before we go out.'

He opened the door to his apartment and stood to one side to let her go in first. 'Here we are.'

'Nice!' said Alba. 'It's kind of normal, not what I expected.'

Jake grinned. 'You didn't expect my flat to be normal? What did you think you'd find? Antique furniture, silk drapes?'

'No, I thought it would be like something styled by a design expert, like you see sometimes in magazines. You know, only pale non-colours like grey and beige, white leather furniture perhaps, one huge painting, no books or magazines lying around. Or perhaps one very glossy magazine.'

'Christ no! I couldn't stand it,' said Jake briskly. 'Too designer for me. Now, how about that lipstick?'

'Oh, of course I can wipe it off. Linley told me to keep the lipstick in this little bag in case I want to re-apply it in the restaurant. So funny! I've never put on lipstick anywhere apart from in my bedroom, not ever. But Linley knows these things, she goes to proper restaurants a lot – she married a guy from that kind of family and they both have terrific jobs. Have you got a tissue?'

'Wow!' she said a few minutes later, standing with Jake's arms around her and nearly breathless from the passion of his kiss. 'You're a demon kisser, Mr Boss-man. Top class, let's do it again.'

'I want to do this first.' He ran a fingertip along the slot in the front of her dress and she felt her face colour as her skin tingled.

'Oh God, don't!' she exclaimed. '*Please* don't do that. We won't get out of here in time for dinner if you do things like that.'

'I know, we'd better stop right now, or we'll be in trouble.'

He got his phone out and called a taxi, and Alba went to the bathroom, reapplied her lipstick and returned to find him standing vacantly looking at the phone still in his hand. In Alba's mind a quick sequence of various reasons for this strange look appeared, none of them good.

'Is something wrong? You look weird.'

His attention snapped back, and he smiled. 'Nothing's wrong. I just realised that I'm happy. Right now, in this place and at this moment I am happier than I've ever been in my life.'

She felt a smile forming. 'Get used to it, Mr Sexy Beast, this is your new normal. Do you like my bag?'

Instinctively she knew that they might get seriously side-tracked if the conversation continued on emotional lines, and she'd have to put another lot of lipstick on and then they'd be late at the restaurant.

'It's lovely,' said Jake and took it out of her hand. 'Mother-of-pear tiles, very pretty. What did it cost?'

'Why do you want to know?'

He grinned and headed for the front door still holding the bag. 'Not out of nearly-but-not-quite husbandly curiosity, you little bully. Just because I thought I should pay for it if it was hideously expensive. It looks expensive, and I know you're funnelling a big portion of your income into that mortgage.'

'Oh, OK then,' said Alba as they got into the lift

which was still at their floor. 'It cost twenty-nine dollars and ninety-five cents in an import shop at Sylvia Park where they sell copies of famous bags and stuff. And it's not real mother-of-pearl, I wouldn't think - probably plastic. But I liked the look of it with the national debt dress.'

She could see the question in Jake's eyes and laughed when he asked, 'Is that how you think of it?'

'Kind of, and it's what I said to my dad, it cost about the same as the national debt. But I promise I won't say that tonight – I'll act very cool.' She looked at herself in the mirror-clad inside of the lift door and smiled at Jake standing behind her looking at her back. 'And don't you dare pull that zipper down! I promise, you can do it later and I can hardly wait, but now's not the right time.'

'I'll keep my hands in my pockets.'

Alba laughed and thought of the silicon uplifters and wondered what he would say when he saw those.

26

When Jake and Alba arrived at The Grove they found John and his wife already installed at a table in the bar with drinks in front of them. Alba suddenly felt nervous, but Jake put his hand on the small of her back and moved her forward with gentle pressure.

'John and Margaret, good to see you! Let me introduce my fiancée, this is Alba.'

'Congratulations! I didn't know you got engaged,' said John and looked appreciatively at Alba. 'This must be very recent. I've seen nothing about it in the media.'

Jake looked at Alba and she gave him a little smile back and let him answer. 'We've been together for a quite a while, but Alba prefers to stay out of the limelight.'

Then from behind them a happy voice exclaimed, 'Alba! Congratulations! I never thought you two would get around to it.'

Alba swung around and was instantly hugged by a short, chubby woman, who whispered in her ear, 'I'm Monica.'

'Monica!' said Alba when she was released from the hug, 'and Pete, hi! Yes, isn't it nice? We just decided over lunch the other day that it was time to get engaged. How are the children? Are they over that tummy bug?'

'Thank God, yes,' said Monica. 'A never to be repeated experience I hope. Hi John, I haven't seen you for ages. You must introduce me to your wife.'

'I would have,' said John,' if you hadn't been so busy hugging Alba.' He turned to his wife. 'Margaret, these people who just arrived are Monica and Pete, old friends of Jake's who I've met once before. At the last MoreIT annual general meeting, I think.'

From there the evening proceeded like any other dinner with friends, but now and then the agreed-on script was introduced into the conversation. When they were studying the menu, Pete turned to Alba and said, 'And by the way, Sarah loves that book on origami you gave her. Sheets of A4 disappear out of the printer and reappear in the form of origami all over the house. You must come and see it.'

Alba smiled, well aware of John looking at her from across the table even when he was talking to someone else. 'I've always liked origami myself, traces of my ancestry, I suppose like this dress - I call it my sushi dress. You know, black wrapping and chopsticks in my hair.'

Everyone laughed. Alba met Jake's eyes, read the silent message of amusement after a brief flash of worry a second earlier, which she felt sure had been when he wondered if she was going to refer to her dress as the national debt dress.

'But tell us, please,' said John halfway through the meal, 'where did you and Jake meet? I've never heard the slightest whisper about this.'

'It was strictly business to start with. He'd heard about me from someone and called to ask for advice about a business proposal he wasn't quite happy about,' said Alba, as agreed with Jake beforehand. 'And then he decided to hire me on a retainer, just for the odd thing now and then, and it went from there. And now I'm thinking about giving up my other contracts.'

'Are you?' asked Pete, sounding surprised. 'I thought your mix of jobs was the perfect thing for you, different people and different settings, no routine.'

Alba turned to him and made a face. 'It *was* the perfect mix, but now Jake's going to nominate me as a director at the AGM, to replace the one who's retiring, so I think I'll have to stop being a secret agent. I'll become too well known to quietly do undercover jobs for others.' She laughed. 'My cover will be blown, just like in a spy movie.'

John's face showed no emotion, but Alba felt a chilly wave of rancour coming towards her, not the dread feeling but a strong current of anger and resentment.

'You must have an impressive background for someone your age,' he said lightly with no hint in his voice of what he was really feeling. 'What kind of thing is it you advise businesses on? What's your background?'

Alba looked at him for a very long silent moment, aware that the others were paying close attention, then she said candidly, 'I have no training whatsoever, apart from an unfinished business degree, but I seem to have a talent for assessing people's motivations. I get asked to sit in on meetings because sometimes I can read a face or a voice better than other people in the room. One of my employers, if you can call them that, a CEO of a listed company, calls me his truth filter.'

'I don't suppose you'd tell us who that was?' said Jake. 'It's a great phrase – and I know how true it is.'

'Don't be silly!' Alba laughed. 'Would you like me to reveal the jobs I've done for you? I know how to keep my employers' secrets.'

'Oh my God, you're psychic!' exclaimed Margaret with gleaming eyes, excited and avid for more. 'It sounds unreal. I've never met anyone like you before. Are you always right?'

'No, certainly not, and I'm not psychic or anything fancy. I just have a talent for knowing when people lie, or when they have hidden motives, as in one case just recently. But I also seem to feel hidden emotions very strongly, however well someone masks their expression and voice. It can be quite uncomfortable, strong dislike or resentment for example.' She let her gaze sweep over John's face and felt Jake's surprise like an unspoken question in her mind.

Monica interrupted, as if she thought this conversation was going off-script and might end up going too far. 'I know you're a wizard at what you do, but to divert you away from business talk - you must tell me where you got that dress! I've been trying to place it ever since you turned around when we first arrived, and I just got it. Apart from the slot it's very like the one Audrey Hepburn wears on that famous movie poster! With long black gloves and a cigarette in a long holder, the ultimate in elegance. Even the hairstyle.'

'Jake bought it for me just recently,' said Alba. 'I never buy expensive clothes, as you know, but he decided to give me a treat. And you're right about the look, the designer called the dress Moon River after the song in that movie.' She looked at Jake. 'I didn't tell you, did I? My mum used to sing that song, but I never knew it came from a film until we bought this dress.'

'Breakfast at Tiffany's – probably one of the most famous movie posters of all time,' said Jake, 'but I will always call it the letterbox dress.'

At the end of the evening, after saying polite goodbyes to John and his wife, who left in a taxi,

Monica turned to Alba. 'Well done, you were perfect! Nobody could have acted being the new fiancée better than you did.'

Ah, thought Alba, Jake hasn't told them we really are engaged, how funny! Won't they be surprised when they find out!

'Classy performance! You'll will charm the whole AGM, I'm sure. The way you made that long pause before you replied to John's questions – classic!' Pete grinned. 'My God, it was just the right signal. He didn't have any idea what Jake was planning for you, which I suppose will happen now?' He gave Alba a searching look. 'I mean, you're really going to be on the board, aren't you? But even with Jake putting you up for a seat on the board, John might still have a go at getting enough votes on his side, I suppose. And getting someone to nominate him is easy.'

'But what if he *does* get enough of those minor shareholders behind him, couldn't their votes combined with his own get him on?' Monica looked at Jake. 'Could he do that? Would he get enough?'

They all looked at Jake who was standing slightly to one side looking down at it his phone and made no reply. He must have told them enough for them to realise what his plan was and why, thought Alba, and that's why they've agreed to be part of this charade tonight, but it's only fair they realise that this isn't a fix, it's just a shot in the air to make a statement.

'I'm sure John understands that if Jake

nominates me and makes sure the shareholders know I've got his support, it will work, or I hope it will,' said Alba. 'We only need to get enough of the minor shareholders to back me and it's OK. And hopefully I'll get your backing as well.'

Jake still hadn't commented on anything they had said since John and Margaret left, but now he looked up.

'OK!' he said energetically and put the phone in his pocket. 'We've got it. Between my shareholding, and yours and Alba's, we now have a majority that John can't beat by forming a voting bloc. You've bought a lot of shares in the last couple of days, Alba, and the number of small shareholders is not what it was.' He chuckled. 'Must have been the price you offered. The little guys couldn't resist.'

'And when are you going to reveal you're not really engaged?' asked Monica who has looked thoughtful for a moment, and slightly worried. 'Won't it seem crazy that you get on the MoreIT board and then you break of the pretend engagement?'

Jake took a step closer to Alba and put his arm over her shoulders, pulled her up against his side and chuckled. 'It's not pretend – it's for real. When I first told you of this idea I never thought she'd want it to be a real engagement. I mean, look at the age difference! But here we are, really and truly engaged.'

The hugs, kisses and exclamations that followed attracted the attention of the barman who had clearly heard enough to understand what they were so happy about. He came out from behind the bar and said, 'Congratulations, Mr Tobin! How about a complimentary glass of champagne to end the evening with?'

27

As soon as the taxi door had closed around them Alba said urgently, 'Jake! How much did you spend – or how much did the trust spend? And is it legal?'

'Totally legal,' said Jake. 'Those shares were bought by the Alba Asher Trust, and you are the beneficiary and soon a trustee, so you can use those shares to vote at the AGM. And it doesn't matter how much I gave to the trust. It achieves two things, John can't get on the board and whatever happens in the future you benefit, so it's all good.'

'Why did you set up the trust without asking me? I've been wondering ever since you told me about it – did you think I might say no?'

'It was the best way to make things work and I had to do something fast. Think of it, now that John knows about you, he might try to buy up as many shares as he can, so I thought we'd get in first. Or he might contact as many shareholders as he can and try to get them on his side – which is now useless. I made myself a trustee and as soon as we've formally added you and Steve – which will happen before the AGM - I'll resign as a trustee and it's nothing to do with me any longer. It's yours alone.'

She stared at him for a moment, trying to take it all in and then she started to laugh. 'You're insane! What a gamble you made giving all that money to the trust – not that I'd ever leave you, but still.'

Before he had time reply, Alba suddenly realised a consequence of their engagement that she couldn't believe she hadn't thought of earlier. 'Oh no! What *are* we going to say when I meet Adam? You said he's been a shareholder from the very start along with Pete, so he'll be at the AGM, won't he? And he'll recognise me, and it will seem crazy, and then he'll resent you for tricking him. What did you tell him after that meeting in the bar?'

Jake clasped her hand in a warm grip. 'Don't worry, it's sorted. I asked him to meet me a couple of days later and said I wasn't interested in their proposal, and he asked why, of course, and said how disappointed he was. So, I said I didn't trust his mate, and then I told him you're actually a close friend of mine, not a schoolgirl, and you're really good at reading faces and people's intentions. I said you got a strong vibe that I should stay out of it.'

'Didn't he think it was a sneaky thing to do? To have me pose as a schoolgirl? What did he say?'

'He had a go at me, yes, but I just said that you've sat in on meetings with me for a while and you're a real asset. And, of course, I implied that whatever Adam's mate had in mind must be something underhand, which made him take a step back. All's fair in love, war and business.'

He chuckled and added before Alba had time to reply. 'Not that I knew at the time that we'd ever end up like this, with your special talent official and being gossiped about right now, as I'm sure it is because John, and particularly Margaret, will be spreading the word. But I thought if I gave Adam the picture he'd understand what I didn't say out loud – that you felt he was in some devious plan with his mate. So, it's all good. Adam will never be a trusted friend again, and he knows that, but you can treat him any way you like next time you meet him. You could refer to the meeting at that bar and make a joke out of pretending to be a schoolgirl and ask him how Georgia is doing at school, or elaborate on the story you told John, or just ignore the whole thing – pretend it never happened.'

Alba sat quietly thinking about this, that it might work to make a joke out of it and have it out in the open, because now Adam knew that she didn't trust him there was nothing he could object to. The last thing she wanted was to be seen as someone who came between Jake and his friends, even the ones he had moved from the close friend zone, but he seemed very relaxed about it.

. . .

'That resentment reference you made, when you mentioned that you could pick up hidden feelings,' said Jake as they got into the lift. 'Did you get the dread feeling from John when you said I was making you a company director? You looked so calm, and I sensed no anxiety from you.'

'Oh no, it wasn't dread, it was just a blast of anger with a strong component of resentment coming at me, impossible to miss, so I thought I'd drive the point home and make sure he knew I'd felt it - that he can't hide from me however good he is at masking his feelings. That's why I mentioned resentment specifically.'

A disconcerting silence followed this statement and after a moment Alba looked up at Jake. 'What's wrong?'

'I had no idea you could feel those things as well! I thought it was only the dread feeling when something bad might happen. When John asked what your training is and what you do, and you mentioned that you could pick up on hidden feelings, I thought you were making it up.'

Waiting for Jake to unlock the door Alba looked at his profile, thought how much she wanted to touch him and pulled herself back to the conversation with an effort.

'What do you mean – making it up? Why would I make it up? I'm just like everyone else, but I think I pick things up more easily. You know how you get what people feel when it's a strong feeling, even if they don't show it?'

'No,' he said bluntly as they walked inside. 'I would never know what someone secretly felt if their face or voice didn't give some hint of it. And looking at John's face I would never have guessed he felt resentment. Never! He seemed perfectly calm and relaxed. Another special talent that probably nobody else has – my God, Alba, what will you come out with next?'

Alba laughed and reached up to pat his cheek. 'Whatever! Doesn't matter if anyone else can, but I think I mostly know when people are lying or hiding emotions. Doesn't matter how well they try to conceal it. Linley knows about me picking up on people lying and says it's uncanny, but she thinks it's probably something I see in their face or their eyes that others don't notice. She keeps going on about how the size people's pupils change when they tell lies – she's a psychology major.'

'Does she know you get what people feel?'

'I've never mentioned it,' said Alba slowly. 'Or I don't think I have because right up to this moment I thought everyone was more or less the same. And I don't think she and I have ever talked about how sensing lies is a nearly physical sensation either, which it is - and she knows nothing about the dread feeling, of course, only dad and you know. The first time I ever told anyone about it was when I realised dad didn't understand what I meant after the interview at your office – when I told him why I had left so suddenly.'

Alba smiled at Jake's still disconcerted face. 'And

about sensing people's feeling - it's like it was with you from the first time I met you. How else do you think I'd have dared be so outrageous and cheeky? I could feel how you enjoyed being teased and bullied even when your serious business face was in place. It was like little currents of warm air washing over me.'

Standing there in Jake's bedroom looking at each other the expression on his face made Alba laugh. 'Jake, this is so weird – here we are, and I'm finally in a place where I can pounce on you and knock you over, but what are we doing? Discussing boring things! You think all that stuff is new and fascinating, and I just thought it was pretty much normal. Don't you want me to ravish you?'

And then, just as he reached for her took a step back. 'Oh no, sorry – I forgot! I've got to get this gunk off my face first.'

She picked up her overnight bag and went into the bathroom and he followed. 'You're not going to pee, are you? OK, good – I just want to see how you do this.'

Alba put a make-up bag beside the handbasin and unzipped it. 'I hope it works! I've never had this kind of make-up on before. Look, here's the magic water, she bought for me - it's got invisible oil in it. Oh no, I haven't got any cotton pads! I told Linley I'd buy some and I forgot. Have you got any?'

'I don't even know what cotton pads are,' said

Jake and handed her a clean facecloth from a shelf full of towels. 'Use this.'

He remained standing just behind her while she washed the make-up off her face and then, when she had finished, he slowly pulled the zip at the back of her dress right down and slid it off her shoulders. Alba met his eyes in the mirror and heard his indrawn breath. His warm hands slid around her ribcage, and she watched in the mirror as he peeled the uplifters off, then his hands cupped her breasts. She trembled as a current of desire flowed down her body from his hands. When she leaned back against him she felt his body's reaction to what he was doing, and she moaned. In a strangled voice he said, 'Don't bother pouncing on me, I'll just carry you to bed.'

Alba woke at three in the morning and after lying awake for a while with Jake's arm holding her against him, she wriggled around under his arm to face him and said, 'Jake, wake up, I need to ask you something.'

'What?' he said sleepily. 'Are you ok?'

'Are we really engaged?' asked Alba, who was now sitting up, wide awake and had flicked the bedside light on. She looked down at his amused face. 'I mean, are we really going to I *continue* being engaged? It was all so sudden, and now I feel as if I rushed you into it by asking if it was for real or pretend.'

Jake reached up and turned the light off before he pulled her down and put an arm around her again. 'You didn't rush me into it. I dreamed of this happening long before you made your stunning love declaration. I just didn't think it ever would. And no, of course, we're not going to be engaged on a continuing basis. I think we should get married unless you don't want to.'

'OK, good,' said Alba and titled her head back to plant a kiss his jaw. 'Just wanted to make sure I hadn't bullied you into it.'

Over breakfast Alba looked seriously at Jake. 'You can tell me to stop any time, you know. I mean, stop me playing silly games. I don't want you to feel I'm not acting serious enough, or adult enough, or something.'

He gave her a long silent look across the breakfast counter, where she was sitting on a tall stool on one side, and he stood on the other. After scrutinising her face for a minute, he said, 'What's this about? Why do you think I might want you to act serious and grown-up all of a sudden?'

'I just thought it might get annoying, so if it does, just tell me to stop. I've always played these silly games at home with my parents, but not ever with anyone else until I met you. But you'll probably get tired of it.'

'Do you remember what I said the first time we met?' asked Jake and put two slices of bread in the toaster.

'Maybe – oh, yes, I think you told me off.'

'Definitely not! All the telling off was done by you. No, I mean do you remember what I asked you to promise after you told me Kipling's story about the elephant's child?'

And she did, it was the first sign of anything unusual, apart from her feeling that she had always known this stranger, and that unbeknownst to either of them they had been close for a long time.

'You asked me to promise I'd never change,' she said slowly. 'Such a strange thing to ask, and I couldn't work out what you meant. I've thought about it a lot ever since. The way you said it and the way you looked at me, it seemed significant, but I didn't know what you were thinking - one of the few times some deep emotion didn't come through.' She paused for a moment while studying his face. 'But perhaps at that stage you were careful not to reveal your interest, kind of guarding your feelings?'

'Exactly right. And you did promise. You said something like "OK boss-person, I promise", didn't you?'

'That's probably right. I was so outrageous the first few times we met. I cringed later when I thought of how rude and cheeky I was.' She paused for a moment before she added, 'But even though I felt as if I'd known you forever from the very beginning, and I could tell you were having fun too behind that façade of yours, I *was* scared I'd gone too far a couple of times. I worried you'd get angry, and I'd never see you again.'

'Now listen to me,' said Jake and put a piece of toast on her plate and one on his own. 'Firstly, and I've already told you this, but in case you didn't believe me – I could never be angry with you. I don't think I'd be able to whatever you said or did. And also, when I asked you never to change, it was because I thought you were the most perfect human being I'd ever met. Funny and cheeky and very clever, not to mention cute. And I hoped that life, or serious, boring people wouldn't ever take those qualities out of you and train you to be just like everyone else. I love you exactly the way you are.'

'OK,' said Alba and paused to study what he had put out to have on their toast. 'I mean, thank you, and I love you the way you are too, *exactly* the way you are, and particularly the way you make me feel – all the time, in bed and out of it. Please don't ever change. I hope you'll love me forever. Don't you have any jam?'

'No, but we can get some if you like. And would you please confirm that you realise that promise I asked for was serious, not just a passing idea. That I'll never ask you to stop being exactly as you are, because you make me laugh more than anyone ever did before, and everything you say is smart, and sometimes shocking and funny at the same time – which is probably very good for me.'

'I do believe it now,' said Alba and got up. 'I'll continue to be my real self, but only with you and dad.' She rounded the breakfast counter, picked up the marmalade jar from the open pantry and reached up to kiss Jake's chin. 'I'll love you forever – there's another promise. And don't you think we're really good at sex together? We hadn't even practised! So, what are we going to do now?'

'You mean right now? As in, go back to your place and tell Steve everything that happened last night?'

Alba wagged her finger at him. 'Now, you listen to me, Mr Nearly-husband-person! We're *not* telling him everything that happened last night. Do you really want to watch his face when I tell him how you took all my clothes off and spread me out like a starfish on the bed and …?'

'God, no! Stop it! But I think we should go back to your house, have a cup of coffee with Steve, tell him an edited version of last night, and kind of plan where to go from here. Like, do you want to tell your friends or family first, should we go out for a meal or have an engagement party – or what?'

'I don't even know how many are in your family, Jake. I've only just realised – all I know is that you have a brother whose wife is called Samantha. Who else?'

'One mother, no father – he disappeared when I was ten or so, went off to find himself and never returned, then died a few years ago. One brother called Dion, his wife Sam and the regulation two kids, both girls. Dion owns a medium-sized trucking and earth-moving company on the North

Shore. A couple of uncles and aunts and a bunch of cousins. We could have a party, or we could just quietly be engaged and invite them to the wedding. Or have a tiny wedding in private and then have a party for everyone a while later and surprise them. What do you think?'

Alba, put her elbows on the breakfast bar and put her hands over her temples and thought for a few minutes, while Jake studied her pose. 'Why do you do that? Look down and rest your head in your hands like that? Does it help you think?'

She looked up and grinned. 'You might not believe this, but when I'm with you and I need to think, I find the only way of avoiding picking up potential strong emotions from you is to sit like that. I'm not resting my head in my hands - I'm holding me head down so I can't look up at you and get distracted.'

'Christ, Alba! Will I ever be able to have any secrets again? Do you feel everything I feel?'

'Don't be silly, of course I don't! Just strong emotions and for some reason when you're amused - I think I always pick that up. That's how I knew when it was OK to tease you some more, even when we first met – all those warm swirls coming towards me.'

'Don't forget the abuse you hurled at me, there was a fair amount of that too, so there must have been the occasional cool breeze too. I was terrified half the time.'

'Haha, very funny,' said Alba and licked

marmalade off her fingers. 'You're such an idiot sometimes – don't forget that most of the time I'll know when you lie.'

An hour later they turned into Church Street and Alba suddenly said, 'Oh please stop! He's at the gate!'

Surprised, Jake pulled in and stopped, and Alba said, 'I won't be a minute, but I've got to hi to him.' There was her Labrador friend at the gate and as soon as he saw who was running towards him he got up on his hind legs with his front paws on the gate, his tail wagging excitedly.

'How are you today? I never usually see you on a Saturday,' said Alba and rubbed his shoulders with both hands. 'Soon I won't be coming past nearly every weekday and I'm going to miss you, big boy.' She leaned over and put her forehead against his and as usual he turned his head a little and licked her wrist.

'A close friend of yours?' said Jake when she got back into the car. 'I could see I've got a rival there.'

Alba giggled. 'Not a rival I'd ever go to bed with though. He's nearly too affectionate – likes to lick me, which isn't my favourite thing. But I've stopped by his gate nearly every weekday morning and evening for over a year now, and we always have a chat. He's such a lovely dog – I do hope his owners appreciate him and give him lots of love.'

. . .

Sitting at the kitchen table with Steve and Jake Alba felt as if her entire existence has shifted slightly sideways since she left the house the previous evening. She was in transition, but there was no definitive point to transition to. Some fixed points of reference would be good, she thought, as she half listened to Jake explaining to Steve how Alba had handled John over dinner.

'And handled is the word. Just like she told me at an early stage,' he said. 'She said she'd handled me surreptitiously from the start, she said she was so skilled at it that I just hadn't noticed. Stealth influence, I think it's called.'

'Nothing would surprise me now!' Steve looked at Alba and shook his head in disbelief. 'Here you are, very nearly twenty-five years old and I'm finding out things I never suspected. Wouldn't Mary have loved all this? The dread feeling, picking up strong emotions from people who're virtual strangers, knowing what's hiding behind expressionless faces. What next?'

'Just what I said.' Jake looked seriously at Steve, who was still staring at Alba, with a bemused look on his face. 'You realise what my life's going to be like now, don't you? I can't hide anything from this little demon, she reads me like a book. Who knows, she might see my dreams at night – it's a scary prospect.'

'You two are just a couple of old, alarmist white guys,' said Alba and started to laugh. 'What *is* the matter with you? Nothing's changed, it's what I've always been like, my half-Korean self or wherever it came from. If it hasn't worried you up to now, then it doesn't matter, does it? Now listen to this, I've made a plan, so let's see what you think about it. We're supposed to discuss what comes next, but all you two do is chatter away about how scary I am.'

She got up and walked to the bench to refill the electric jug. 'I'll make another cup of tea and tell you at the same time. I think we should have a little dinner party here first, so we can tell the people who matter in a home setting, not a restaurant. We can squeeze eight people around that table if they're not too fat. So, how about us three, Jake's mum and his brother, sister-in-law plus two kid – that's eight. I'll cook something nice. And then we can have Linley and Zac for a drink or dinner another night – they're the only ones I want to pre-warn, so they don't feel left out when we tell people we're getting married.'

'And how and when are you getting married? Have you decided?'

'We thought we might sneak off and do it very quietly, but I'm not so sure now.' Jake looked a question in Alba's direction. 'I know your Korean relations might not come all this way, but don't you think uncles and aunts and whatever, and you friends Linley and Zac would like to celebrate with us instead of at a party later on?'

'Plenty of time,' said Steve. 'We can put it on the back burner and discuss it when we've had time to think.'

29

When Alba texted Linley to say she would call in after work, if they were going to be in, because she had something important to tell them, Linley fired back a text so fast that Alba hadn't even had time to put the phone back in her pocket.

Good news or bad? You've got me worried.

All good, no need to worry!

She was taken aback by this fast reaction and couldn't understand why Linley had reacted so strongly, but it was a busy day in the warehouse, and she had no time to spare for further text exchanges. That morning, when she had decided she must tell Linley and Zac without a further moment's delay, she had blessed the fact that she still had her mother's car. For some reason neither Steve nor she had got around to doing anything about selling it, and now it meant she wouldn't have to take two different buses crammed with people going home from work. As she continued picking and packing she mentally planned the easiest detour to a supermarket on the way to Linley's, so she could pick up a bottle of wine and some nibbles on the way without getting caught in some endless trap of waiting for an onramp to clear. It went without saying that the visit would become festive, as nearly everything did at their place, so providing both the reason and the supplies seemed like a nice idea.

Mid-afternoon Mark came to find her, looking stressed and carrying a clipboard. 'I'm sorry, Alba,' he said between panting breaths after hurrying to one of the furthest aisles. 'The courier truck is coming forty-five minutes early for some reason. I don't know what's up with them these days, always changing the pick-up time – they must be trying new routes or something. Can you bring what you've packed now and then continue right up until they get here? God knows, we don't need this on a day with so many orders.'

They hurried back towards the loading dock with Mark panting beside Alba who pushed the trolley at a half run. 'God, you're fit!' he exclaimed when they got there. 'It's all that running to and from work, I suppose. Look at me, I'm nearly dead on my feet.'

Alba smiled and refrained from pointing out that he was thirty years older and probably weighed fifteen kilos more than he should.

'Yeah, the running does keep me fit,' was all she said and started unloading boxes and piling them up with what they had already packed that day. 'I'll grab another box of shredded paper and go straight back and see how much more I can pack before they come. Just text me when they're here and I'll come back with what I have.'

She turned just as she was about to jog back with her trolley. 'Do you want me to find the other guys and tell them to come over now, or have you already told them?'

'I've told them.' Mark and wiped his arm across his forehead. 'I'll grab a trolley and go around and collect their stuff now. And thanks for reminding me – I'll take some shredded paper and parcel tape as well in case they're running short.'

Concerned about how red and sweaty Mark looked, and working faster than ever, Alba had no time to think about anything other than the next items on her list, and which would be the quickest to get to first. She put parts in boxes, filled them with shredded paper and taped them up as fast as she could and started on the next order. By the time Mark's text arrived, saying the truck was there, she had six boxes taped up and with labels stuck on. She ran full tilt down the central aisle pushing the big flatbed trolley in front of her and got there just as the courier driver was putting the last box from the pile in his truck.

'Good work, team!' said Mark as they stood watching the truck drive away. 'I don't think we've ever got so much done so fast before. How about a beer at five?'

Alba started turning her trolley around. 'Thanks, nice idea, but I've got an appointment straight after work.'

'Engaged!' exclaimed Linley and came to a sudden stop in the middle of the living room when Alba made her announcement. She stared at the bottle in Alba's hand with a dismayed look. 'To Ludo?'

Alba burst out laughing and the increasingly slippery bottle of sparkling wine started sliding from her grasp, but Zac quickly grabbed it before it fell. Alba didn't even notice, she was laughing so hard and the other two stared, first at her then at each other. Linley took the bag out of Alba's hand and put an arm around her.

'Alba, come and sit down and tell me what's wrong, you seem overwrought. What's happened? This isn't like you.'

'Nothing's wrong, everything is perfect, and I might be the happiest person in the world! I just couldn't believe you'd think I'd *ever* get engaged to Ludo of all people!'

'Why not?' asked Zac, still standing there with the bottle dripping condensation on the carpet and a confused expression on his face. 'What's wrong with Ludo? He seemed like a nice bloke.'

Alba turned back to face Zac. 'Listen Zac, Ludo is not only very, very boring, he's also got *no* imagination and *no* intuition, he doesn't read real books, he has no interests outside his field of study, and he doesn't get most of my jokes. And as I said the other day to the man I *have* got engaged to, Ludo manages to be clever and stupid at the same time – quite a feat. *Plus*, and this is probably the worst thing, he's a grabber. He thinks if he makes a grab for a girl with no warning and no lead-in, a girl who's given him absolutely *no* encouragement at all, she's going to let him take her to bed. He's an idiot!'

'I suspected he was like that, which is why I might have sounded alarmed. When I saw the way he looked you up and down when I introduced you and the arrogant way he dismissed us, I got bad vibes about him.' Linley shook her head at the memory. 'That look wasn't just appreciation - it was something else and I didn't like it. So, when I thought it might be him I got worried.'

She opened the bag and looked inside it before handing it to Zac. 'Why don't you get some glasses and open that bottle, and we'll sit down with these lovely snacks?'

She turned back to Alba. 'Now then, who did you get engaged to? I mean, you can't come in here, erupt in hysterical laughter, with a bottle of bubbly and nibbles and say you got engaged and let's celebrate - and then not tell us who the man is, can you? It can't be someone we know, or we'd have heard rumours. Where did you meet him and how long has this been going on? And has it got anything to do with that dress?'

Alba pulled her phone out and sat down on the

sofa. 'Of course, I'll tell you who it is, but I it was so funny when you thought it was Ludo that I got distracted. I'll find the photo dad took of us just after he gave us mum's engagement ring, I got him to send it to me so I could show you. And it *was* the day you did my hair when I was going to that dinner I told you about.' She held up her hand and waggled her fingers. 'I don't wear the ring at work because I'm dead scared I'll lose it when I push packaging in around things in the boxes, but I have it in my little zip pocket, and I put it on the moment I leave. It feels as if my mum is with me when it's on my finger, so lovely!'

She found the photo and passed the phone to Linley, who said, 'Oh my God, you've got to come and look at this, Zac!'

Zac put a tray down on the coffee table and crouched beside her chair to look at the photo, then both of them looked at Alba with nearly identical expressions, a mixture of surprise and awe. Alba waited with bated breath for their reactions. These two were her best friends and she was hoping one of them wouldn't say, "Isn't he a bit old for you?"

'Fabulous dress - you look utterly amazing! Who *is* that nice hunk?' said Linley.

'Jesus! That's Jake Tobin!' exclaimed Zac. 'You got engaged to Jake Tobin! How the hell did that happen?'

'Oh, well …' said Alba innocently, back in charge now that she had recovered her normal cool. 'We've been meeting for a while for coffee and lunch and things, and I've been helping him with some business stuff, and then one day we were in a café, and he asked me to marry him, so I said "yes, please". And then he took me outside and kissed me for several minutes in the rain, and we got absolutely soaked. And then we went back inside and had coffee and carrot cake. And then we went and bought the Moon River dress, and then we went out for that dinner and then we went back to his place and then we … Oh no, sorry Zac - I don't think I'll tell you that part, it's still a bit new and private.'

Linley shook her head and looked at Zac who was still crouching beside her chair staring at the phone. 'So, who is this Tobin guy? He looks vaguely familiar.'

'Babe, really? You don't know? I don't believe it,' exclaimed her husband. 'He built up MoreIT from scratch, it's worth untold millions or billions and so is he. And where Alba met him I can't imagine. He's got a reputation for being super cool, very clever and very private. I think he's the most desirable bachelor in town, or *was*, I suppose I mean.'

Alba leaned over and took the phone back, cast a fond look at Jake and said, 'I'll tell you the whole tale, how it really happened, but I've got to text dad first and tell him I'll be late, because it's a long story. And just so you know, Jake reads real books, and he gets all my jokes, and he's not a grabber – and he's kind. I love him so much that just talking about him makes me nearly breathless.'

When she left at quarter to eight, they had eaten all the snacks she had brought, Linley and Zac had finished the bottle of wine after Alba had half a glass and then stuck to water as she always did, and the entire story had been told from the first call from Jake to the strategic dinner.

'You see, the dress was part of the truth filter mission,' she explained after deciding that she would tell them the story in all its parts by replacing the dread feeling with her ability to tell when people lie, because telling them about the dread feeling was not something she could even contemplate. Now that she was beginning to believe that very few, or maybe no others ever got the dread feeling, she didn't want it discussed any further; Jake and Steve were the only two she would ever tell and nobody apart from Jake would ever know about the man on the bus.

'And it's not that I can tell when they lie all the time,' she emphasised to Linley, who was listening to the description of the dinner with her eyes wide. 'I can sometimes, as you know, and Jake calls me his truth filter, because it's twice now I've picked up on it that someone's lying to him when he didn't realise.'

As she drove home through the now quieter streets, she thought how well it had worked to avoid any details about the fraud saga by simply saying that she had aborted the interview because she felt she was being lied to. It had meshed nicely with why Jake had called her in the first place; because he was intrigued and wanted to know why she had walked out.

'I've been very devious and lied to my best friends, which is both sad and bad,' said Alba out loud in the empty car, 'but I had to make it credible without giving anything away, didn't I? Telling Linley and Zac the whole saga was important, and surprisingly not even Zac linked it in any way to the fraud news from MoreIT a couple of months ago. And I avoided mentioning that the Winterdale woman was part of the interview, and they didn't ask what kind of job I had applied for. Perfect!'

She was relieved and amused in equal parts, both at her own skill in avoiding the pitfalls and at their reactions, particularly Zac's. She had wondered if his work as a financial analyst for an investment company would set up a chain reaction in his head, but luck had been on her side and there had been no need for further evasions.

30

It was the morning of the day Alba thought of as Family Dinner Day, a sunny Saturday and surprisingly warn for the season. Alba and Jake were having a mid-morning coffee in the garden before starting on the next stage of chores, Steve was playing with the band at a food fair and Jake had spent the first part of the morning mowing the lawn.

'I'm going to break our contract,' said Jake. 'I don't want to be my wife's employer - it feels totally wrong.'

'Oh,' said Alba and then stopped, as if she were thinking of something else.

Jake continued quickly, 'If you want to work at the company that's fine, there are plenty of things you could get involved in half or full time, clever stuff - but to have a contract with my wife and paying her out of my private money seems all wrong now. I really don't want you to call me Mr Boss-person when we're married.'

Oh well, thought Alba, I wonder how this will turn out, but I have one job, and I can get another one until the mortgage is paid off. She looked absently at the plum tree while she thought about how this would impact on their lives. She'd have to work all hours of the week and they'd hardly see each other, apart from late at night, unless she found a really well-paid job.

'Did you hear what I said?' asked Jake. 'Did you drift off?'

'What? Of course not, I'm wide awake, I was just thinking.'

'Did you hear what I said?'

'About breaking the contract? Of course, that's what I was thinking about.'

Jake looked closely at her and shook his head in disbelief. 'My God, I don't believe it - I've never seen you do that before. You didn't hear a word I said after that, did you? What was suddenly so important that you totally tuned me out?'

'The mortgage, of course,' said Alba patiently. 'I was thinking of what second job I could get that wouldn't eat up every hour of my week.'

'Darling Alba, *please* tell me you don't think I expect you to work instead of studying, to pay that bloody mortgage!' Jake's voice held a note of desperation, and she felt his distress like a buffeting of strong wind.

'But I have to,' she said reasonably. 'Dad can't do it on his own now that the weekly payment is so much higher. He just doesn't earn enough, and it wouldn't work.'

Jake reached out and captured her hand and held it tight. 'You're such a little fighter! I've already sorted it out with Steve, I should have told you that first up – I'm sorry! I'm giving him the money to pay off the mortgage and the penalty interest for breaking the mortgage term early, as a compensation for taking you away and leaving him to live in this house alone *and* for the ring I needed to become engaged to you.'

'You did what!?' said Alba loudly, suddenly energised and scowling ferociously. 'I can't *believe* it - you bought me, you big bully! I've been trafficked, it's illegal.'

'Please don't report me to the UN and get me vilified in global media again! I did *not* buy you. I told him I realised the impact it would have, not having you paying part of the household expenses and helping with the mortgage, and I didn't insult him by mentioning how different his daily life will be without you. And I explained that it doesn't sit well with me to employ my wife with private money, to have you working for me. Helping me is fine, working for me isn't unless you're employed by the company. Which he totally agreed with.' He loosened his tight grip on her and smiled. 'We settled on the phrase "friendly exchange" to make it acceptable to both of us. As I said to him, your mother's ring saved me a fortune for a start. It only took me about an hour to convince him while you were with Linley the other evening after work. I drove out here, and we sat down over a beer and thrashed it out.'

'Don't you want me to continue working?'

'You can do anything you want to, it's up to you, but I thought you wanted to go back to your studies. And once you're on the board of directors you'll be paid for that, of course, just like the other board members – quite a lot. And don't forget the penalty clause in the contract we had until I broke it - and which you obviously didn't read properly.'

He was still holding her hand and she felt the warmth of concern and care in his mind, but still mixed with a small portion of worry like a little dark under-tone. 'Look at it like this, Alba, and try to discount the fact that I left you out of my discussion with Steve, which was stupid. I want you to do the things you most want to do and give you the opportunity to live the life you deserve. It's not about me dictating to you, or you having to do things please me.'

He lifted her hand and kissed her wrist. 'It's about you. You should be free to do things for yourself, not constantly be constrained by helping others as you have done for the last two or three years.'

Alba swallowed hard to prevent a sob escaping and curled her fingers tight around his. 'You are the best thing ever, I'm so lucky!'

'We're both lucky, darling.'

When Jake left, Alba spent the rest of the day cooking and preparing the house for visitors. Last of all she set the table the way her mother used to do it for special occasions, with candles and flowers from the garden. When she finally stood back and surveyed the effect, Steve came up beside her and put his arm around her. 'Mary would be proud of this, Alba. She was always so particular about having the table look nice when we had guests.'

'I was just thinking about her. I tried to do it the same way, but we've got a problem because I can only find seven chairs. Where is the eighth one?'

'Did you take the one in the spare room and the one in my bedroom? OK, we had eight, so one's missing … let me think.'

Alba got it first. 'I know! You put it in the garage last year when we decided to push the table back and we didn't want a chair jammed up against the wall. If you get it, I'll go and have a shower before Jake comes.'

By the time they were having the apricot cheesecake Alba had made from a handwritten recipe she found folded in her mother's favourite cookbook, the evening felt relaxed and casual. Her initial tension when she greeted Jake's family had evaporated. In the days leading up to the Family

Dinner Day, which in her mind always had capital letters because of how important it was for her relationship with the Tobin clan, she had felt increasingly apprehensive. She had wondered if they would disapprove because of the age difference or her mixed race, or because she worked in a warehouse. It wasn't until they arrived that she realised she hadn't thought to ask Jake how much he had told them about her, and by then it was too late.

But now she looked around the table and wondered if her worries had been influenced by Steve telling her about the problems when he and Mary wanted to marry. Tonight, nobody had seemed surprised or upset at Jake's choice. Jake's mother had been introduced as Joanne and instantly made a dismissive gesture at Jake and told Alba and Steve to just call her Jo like all her friends did, and then very quickly revealed her matriarchal side, keeping an eagle eye on her two grandchildren and probably on her two sons as well. Alba watched her interact with her family and felt like laughing. They're all children to her, she thought, even Jake.

'But tell me a bit about how you and Jake met,' said Samantha now and pushed her dessert plate to one side. "Girls, can you please take the plates to the kitchen? Dion and I tried to prise some details out of Jake, but we only got a very sketchy version.'

Jo shook her head at Jake and turned to Alba. 'He's got this privacy thing to the nth degree. I got practically nothing out of him either. You'll have to fill us in, Alba.'

The look she gave Alba was impossible to mistake; the matriarchal authority now extended to her as well. Jake cast a glance loaded with amusement in her direction, and she thought maybe it would be good for his family, who obviously regarded him as a bit overly serious and secretive, to hear about another side.

'It was a bit unusual I suppose. I applied for a job at MoreIT and got short-listed,' she said. 'But I decided not to go through with the second interview even though I was one of two final candidates, so Jake called and asked why I'd walked out of the interview after only a few minutes. Not that he was in the room at the time, but his HR manager had told him. And he asked for us to meet, he was dead set on finding out the reason, but I turned him down. I had to use the unconditional no, that I learnt from a cop who came to our school when I was eight.'

Everyone's eyes were on her now and if the silence was any indication, they were fascinated. Sam and Dion's nine-year-old daughter, Benita stared at Alba with her eyes wide. 'Why didn't you want to meet him?'

'Because I didn't think the reason I walked out of the interview was any of his business. So, I said no and ended the conversation, but then he called again couple of weeks later, and we met for coffee. And he was full of questions, just kept asking me things, so I told him he was just like the elephant's child – and as a warning I asked if he knew what happened to the elephant's child, who also asked endless questions and got into serious trouble.'

She could see the little girl was just about to ask and added quickly, 'After dinner's really finished – when we've had chocolates and maybe coffee – I'll lend you a book about the elephant's child that I had as a little girl and you'll realise it's *very* lucky Jake doesn't have a trunk instead of a nose now.'

Inside she was laughing at the expressions around the table, riveted on her now and waiting for more. She slid a sideways look at Jake and felt his amusement like a warm touch. 'Anyway, that coffee date became very romantic,' she continued, on a roll and turning it into a story. 'I told him off for asking things that were no business of his and threatened to report him to the United Nations for invading my personal privacy, and I told him he's a big bully. Such a romantic date, don't you agree? Just like a movie.'

Her audience was laughing, and Dion said, 'No wonder he fell in love with you. I bet nobody's treated him like that since he was a kid.'

Steve turned to Jake's mother and said in a mock-serious tone, 'As soon as I heard that Miss Bossy had told Jake off in that special way of hers, I asked her how he reacted to being abused, and apparently he told her she was a nasty little bully herself, so it's no wonder we're sitting here tonight. They were clearly made for each other.'

Dion was moving his head slowly from side to side the way people do when they are incredulous, and Alba smiled. Perhaps he hadn't seen this side of Jake since they were children. But she was amazed that nobody has followed up on the start of her story and asked why she walked out of the interview. One of life's mysteries, she thought and made a bet with herself that sooner or later someone would remember and ask her. She made a mental note to tell Jake that replacing the dread feeling with her ability to know when people lied would have to be the way they explained it.

After the promised chocolates, Alba took the girls to her bedroom and read the picture book version of the elephant's child story to them, and then let them stay in her room with one playing Minecraft on her laptop and the younger one playing Blockheads on her phone.

'Be good now, kids,' said Samantha, who had stood in the doorway listening and watching. 'And don't go anywhere else on those devices, no snooping! Just stay in the games.'

She followed Alba back to the living room and said, 'Did you find a dress? I was going to ask Jake and then I forgot. I was very intrigued to have him text and ask for suggestions for classy boutiques, so not him!'

'I'll show you,' said Alba and detoured into the kitchen to pick up Steve's phone from where he always left it on top of the fridge. 'Dad took a photo of us the night we went to that dinner, and I wore my sushi outfit. Here it is.'

Sam took the phone out of her hand and exclaimed, 'Oh my God! You're Audrey Hepburn with a Korean slant – all that's missing are the long gloves. How gorgeous!'

She kept hold of the phone and headed towards the living room and said over her shoulder, 'I can show Dion and Jo, can't I? They'll love it.'

She didn't wait for an answer but walked across the room holding the phone out in front of her.

'You've *got* to see this! Not only have we got a new person in the family – and one who can handle Jake, yay! – but check out what she turns into when she dresses up!'

Alba followed, unable to meet anyone's eyes. Her father was smiling at the sight of Dion and his mother both reaching for the phone as if they were competing about who was going to get it first. Jake walked behind the sofa and put an arm around Alba, who suddenly felt slightly unsettled by all this sudden attention.

'What's the matter? Didn't you want Sam to show them? And that was a great story you told them over dinner,' he said in a low voice covered by the comments and exclamations from the others who were now passing Steve's phone back and forth.

'I know, but this is different, I didn't start it – I'm not in control.' Alba turned under his arm and leaned against him. 'I like having you beside me, it feels so good.'

'Always,' said Jake quietly and smiled down at her. 'I'll always be beside you. And this lot are just excited because you're such a lovely surprise, they're not always like this - they'll calm down shortly.'

When Linley returned Alba's call a couple of days after the family dinner she sounded stressed.

'What's the matter?' asked Alba. 'Is something wrong?'

'No, I'm just flat out at the learning centre, running around trying not to keep anyone waiting. We're having another of those parent and child days when we discuss their various learning difficulties and ways to deal with them. When you work with kids and their parents at the same time, things get side tracked very easily and you end up spending more time than you planned with one lot before you can carry on. But I missed a call from you earlier, so let's get back to that.'

'Can you come for dinner at Jake's place tomorrow night? Just you and Zac – I want you to get to know him before the wedding.'

'When is the wedding? Already? You only just got engaged.'

'I'll tell you everything tomorrow – it's exciting, but I don't want to take up any more of your time now when you're so busy. I'll text you the address.'

How's it going? read the text from Jake later that day. It was Alba's last day in the warehouse, and with two of the three men away, one with a sprained thumb and one on leave, the race to get orders packed in time for the courier truck was frantic.

Crazy busy, talk later. Alba pushed the phone into her back pocket and taped up the box in front of her before she reached for her tablet and started on the next order. When Mark texted that the courier was going to be half an hour late Alba thought she might be able to finish her share of the day's orders provided she worked faster than ever. At ten to five she ran down the central aisle with her trolley and saw the truck reversing up to the loading dock at the far end. Perfect! Now she could feel she had truly finished her work here with nothing left undone.

She had told Mark and the others that she would bring a nice lunch for everyone on her last day and had spent the previous evening making fried rice cakes and kimbap, which she knew the others would be familiar with and simply think of as sushi.

'Ah! Rice cakes,' Steve had said when he came in from work. 'Are there any for me or is it all for your work lunch tomorrow?'

'Lots for us – the spicy ones are for us, and the less spicy ones are for work, and I don't want to mix them up. I don't know how hot they like their food. And I've made lots of kimbap with our favourite fillings and a few other things. Jake's coming over about seven to have dinner with us.'

So now, all she had to do was pick up the empty food containers from their little lunch party and say goodbye.

'I'm really sorry you're going,' said Mark when she was ready to leave. 'You're the best worker I've ever had. The new guy seems OK, but it takes ages to train people. We'll see how he goes - he might turn out OK. And don't forget to pop in for a coffee if you're in the neighbourhood.'

'I've left some food in the fridge for you to share tomorrow,' said Alba. 'Say goodbye to the others for me.'

As she walked to her car she thought how strange it would be not to go to work the next morning, but with the wedding coming up so unexpectedly soon she needed the time to get organised.

When Alba's phone buzzed with a text the following evening Jake picked it up and said, 'It's Linley, they're downstairs now - what should I say? Do you want to go down and bring them up?'

'I'm too busy. Just tell her which floor and press the entry button on your what's-it, please,' said Alba and turned to put the casserole back in the oven, quickly washed her hands and untied her apron.

'God, you look so cute in your big apron. I feel like giving you a hug.'

She flung the apron on a stool by the breakfast counter, took the time for a quick hug and went to open the front door seconds before the lift arrived, and their first dinner guests as a couple had arrived.

After the introductions, Alba went back to the kitchen on the excuse that she needed to check that a pot wasn't boiling too hard, but what she really wanted was for Jake to get acquainted with Linley and Zac without her. She listened to what she could hear from the living room, offers of a glass of wine or a beer and comments about the view, and she smiled at how restrained Zac sounded. She had understood from her last visit that he idolised Jake as a successful businessman and remembered perfectly his awestruck face when she revealed who she was engaged to. By the time she joined them in the living room they were standing by the balcony door looking out over the harbour and she heard Jake say, 'I'll let Alba tell you – there's been so much going on I can hardly keep track of it.'

'Yeah, right!' she said and took the glass Jake handed her. 'As if you'd ever forget anything. Aren't you related to the elephant's child?'

He pulled her in with an arm over her shoulders. 'She keeps me on my toes, never a dull moment.'

Linley's eyes were sparkling now, and she smiled at Jake. 'I had a feeling she would surprise us one day, and when she told us how you let her tease you I knew she'd found the right man. I don't imagine many of your staff treat you like that?'

'I bet they don't dare,' said Alba. 'He's usually quite a serious kind of guy, but that's just camouflage. His secretary loves him, thinks he's the best boss ever. And I'm not on the staff now, he sacked me.'

'So, when exactly is the wedding and why so soon?'

Alba gestured to the armchairs. 'Let's sit down and have some of those snacks I made. Dinner won't be for another hour and if I finish this glass of champagne without anything to eat I'll probably not be able to serve dinner, I'll be asleep. And I'll get a glass of water, back in a moment.'

'So, this is what happened,' she said and sat down on the arm of Jake's chair. 'My hal-abeoji, my grandpa in Korea, is due to have a hip joint replaced and he's very worried about it. He's never been ill in his life, never been in hospital or anything, and he said – and this is the truth – he said he wants to see me married in case he dies during the operation. He's dead scared, so I said, of course we'd get married right away – his operation is booked, and he doesn't want to change the date. I think he needs to get it done and stop fretting about dying, so we're getting married very quickly.'

'The poor guy,' said Jake. 'Steve told me your grandmother said there's no reasoning with him however hard she tries - he's convinced he might die. So, the wedding is in three weeks, and they'll be here for only four days.'

'Elizabeth is helping us organise everything, she seems to know a lot about weddings which is lucky for me because I've only been to one – that was yours.' Alba thought for a moment with a frown. 'Who was that lovely guy who married you?'

'That was Zac and he's still lovely,' said Linley and smiled. 'If you mean who performed the ceremony it was Zac's cousin Alberto, who used to be called Albert, but he decided it was old-fashioned and boring and changed his name. He is a certified marriage celebrant, very popular.'

Zac, who had said very little since they arrived, looked confused. 'Who's Elizabeth?'

'She's my secretary.' Jake chuckled. 'I don't think I've ever seen her so excited about anything in the twelve years she's been with me. Every day she presents us with new choices, first it was venues, then food, then decorations – God knows what will be on my desk in the morning. I pass them on to Alba so those two can discuss things between them or with my sister-in-law, but we're keeping my mother right out of the organising committee, or she would just take over the whole thing. And I don't care about the details, so long as I get to marry this little demon.'

Alba had been waiting for the opportunity to talk privately to Linley and she was beginning to think she wouldn't get it if she didn't deliberately create it. But when they had finished the apple and cinnamon cake dessert and Linley was helping her clear the table Alba quickly pulled her into the corner by the pantry where the men, who were having a deep discussion about Bitcoin, wouldn't hear them.

'This is important,' she said without preamble. 'You know I would have asked you to be my matron of honour, there's nobody I feel as close to, you're like a sister. But we're having no attendants at all. Jake told Dion the same thing I'm telling you, no maid of honour and no best man. You and Zac and Jake's immediate family will be at the head table with us and dad, and my grandparents. And you'll be in the so-called family rows of chairs right at the front during the ceremony.'

'Oh, Alba,' said Linley and hugged her tight. 'I *will* be like family then. And remember how I couldn't ask you to be a bride's maid at my wedding because the mass of cousins and sisters on both sides made things so difficult? Of course, I understand.'

Right at the end of the evening, when Zac had decided they should leave the car and had called for a taxi, Linley suddenly said, 'Alba! My God, have you found a dress? You'll have to buy a ready-made one – I know a fabulous bridal shop.'

'I've got one already,' said Alba with a straight face. 'Dad and I sorted it out - and it's lovely.'

She didn't dare look at Jake and his amusement surrounded her like a swirl of warm air, and she knew he was just about to laugh, so she added quickly, 'Dad wants me to keep it secret, so nobody else is allowed to see it before the wedding, not even Jake though he's been trying to get me to show him. Dad's being very particular about all these traditional things.'

'Well, of course he is,' said Jake. 'His own wedding was just him and your mother in a registrar's office or something, so he wants it to be special. I've been trying to guess what the wedding dress is going to be like, but Alba refuses to give me any clues at all. And by the way, the invitation should be with you tomorrow. We know it's short notice so maybe everyone won't be able to come.'

'Where is it?'

'The Hilton,' said Alba. 'Elizabeth suggested it and we've booked my grandparents in there too, so my hal-abeoji doesn't have to walk far. And the space where we'll have both the ceremony and the dinner is lovely, it's right at the top of the building and overlooks the harbour.'

32

Two days before the wedding, the day before Alba's grandparents were due to arrive, Jake joined her and Steve for lunch.

'Did you take the day off?' asked Steve. 'You're not getting wedding nerves, are you?'

'No way! I thought I might be useful in some way, but Elizabeth assures me everything is under control. She and Sam have discussed the finer details and she says there is nothing to be done now, so I came over to have some company.'

'Don't go into my room and peep at the dress!' said Alba. 'I might go and lock the door - I think I left the wardrobe open.'

'I can't wait to see it. I have high expectations after the last dress I saw you in.' He looked her up and down and smiled. 'The way you can change who you are by getting out of jeans and trainers and putting on smart clothes is amazing, so the wedding dress has me intrigued. And what are the plans for your grandparents?'

'They arrive at half past six tomorrow morning, but they travel first class, so they'll have slept on the flight,' said Alba. 'And they said they don't want to do any sightseeing, they've seen it all already, so why don't we go and have lunch with them at the hotel? That gives them time to unpack and settle in first.' She felt she needed to explain her reasoning to Jake and added, 'It's not that they're terribly old or anything, they're only in their early or mid-seventies, and they've been here four or five times before, but I think my grandfather is reluctant to move around with his crutch. It's not a look that fits his image of himself.'

'I offered to pick them up,' said Steve and grinned at Alba. 'I think you could hear it from where you were sitting next to me at the time – the answer was a strong "no, thanks" so fast I couldn't get a word in. They'd already booked a car to take them straight to the Hilton.'

'OK, I'll email them tonight and say we'll come to the hotel for lunch. And then we can discuss where to from there – find out what they want to do on that one day they have here after the wedding, but they might just want to hang out with us – at the hotel, of course. They've only got one day free and then they're off on Monday morning.'

. . .

As they drove away from the Hilton in the late afternoon the following day, after a long and noisy lunch with Alba's grandparents, Jake looked across at Alba. 'Why was your grandfather laughing so much – were you telling him naughty things or teasing him? And I didn't know you speak Korean, I never thought to ask if you do.'

'My Korean is pretty awful, and quite often I don't get the intonation quite right, so sometimes a word I say comes out as one that means something else. I always practise on him instead of speaking English. He thinks it's very funny and keeps telling me I must only speak English when I'm in Korea or I might end up in a fight when I've accidentally insulted someone.'

Steve leaned forward from the backseat and said, 'But what was it he said to you when he took you aside when we were leaving, Jake? If you don't mind telling us, but it was quite a long conversation.'

Jake met Steve's eyes in the rear vision mirror and chuckled. 'He had obviously lined up a few things, very strategic approach. First he said he'd looked into my background, and that of MoreIT and asked me a few very pertinent business questions, and he said he approved of Alba's choice. Then he told me she hasn't got the pancreatic cancer gene like her mother had and his mother too, he thinks. And last of all he told me a secret.'

'What?! A secret?' Alba was outraged. 'He told

you a family secret or something, instead of telling me?'

'He said he has five grandchildren,' said Jake. 'And you're the eldest.'

Alba looked suspiciously at him. 'That's not a secret. You're making it up! What did he really say?'

'He said you're in his will.'

Alba turned to look at Steve in the backseat with a worried frown. 'I hope he's not losing the plot. I've known I'm in his will since the first time I met him practically. Well, not the first time perhaps, because I was only two years old, but at least since I was ten. He's always told me and the cousins that we'll all get the same, no favourites.'

Jake shook his head. 'I'm quite sure it was a kind of warning for me, so I'd know you're not going to have to depend on me. But why on earth didn't he help you with that mortgage? Did he know about it?'

'Oh, God no!' exclaimed Steve. 'Mary and I never talked about money with her parents, never! Not after they gradually accepted me, and we were getting along fine. We never discussed anything to do with money, so they had no idea we ever had a mortgage I wouldn't think.'

33

The huge glass-walled space on the top floor of the Hilton hotel on Princes Wharf glowed white and silver with two hundred chairs decked out with white covers and huge silver chiffon bows. The white carpet that ran up the centre of the room ended in front of a glass wall, where Jake stood waiting beside an arch of greenery and white flowers.

Alba turned from peeking through a crack in the door and looked wide-eyed at Steve. 'I never imagined I'd have a wedding like this, never! It's like a fairy tale – it must have cost a fortune.'

'It's what Jake wanted,' said Steve calmly. 'He said he wanted to show you off and give you both something wonderful to remember.' Then he laughed quietly and added, 'I never thought you'd have a wedding like this, either. I've never been to anything like this in my life.'

Inside the music started, they stopped talking and looked at each other, then Alba nodded. The two waiters stationed beside the doors opened them, and Alba and her father started their slow walk up the long white carpet. A collective sound like a sigh ran through the room, as if the two hundred guests standing watching them had very quietly whispered "wow" in unison.

Jake's eyes met Alba's and she kept her gaze on him all the way up the aisle, thinking she would remember this moment and the look on his face to her dying day.

They were married by Zac's cousin Alberto and the ceremony went smoothly right up to the point when Alba thought it was finished and was ready to turn around, but Alberto had one more thing to say and looked at Jake. 'And will you love Alba forever?'

She stared at him, startled by this unexpected question that had not been in the script they had agreed on, and Jake replied, 'I will love her with every breath I take from this day forward.'

When they turned around Alba saw her grandmother crying, tissues being pulled out of bags and pockets, and Linley with tears streaming down her cheeks, wiping them away with her fingers. Alba leaned ever so slightly towards Jake and looked up at him. 'Me too,' she whispered and gripped his hand tight.

. . .

In the crush of guests wanting to wish them well, Alba stood beside Jake with a champagne glass containing non-alcoholic sparkling wine. She found herself explaining her traditional hanbok costume over and over and felt her grandmother's emotional attention on her from where she stood a few steps away beside Alba's grandfather and Steve.

After what seemed like an eternity of standing and smiling and endlessly repeating the same things Alba was relieved to hear dinner announced, but just as they were starting to move towards the head table Morgan and his wife approached.

'Congratulations!' he said and kissed her cheek then shook hands with Jake while Alba's aunt admired her hanbok and said what a wonderful surprise it had been to see her in it instead of a white wedding dress.

'It was important to dad and me,' said Alba seriously. 'We feel it honours my mother and my ancestry to wear it. My grandmother bought it for mum when she graduated, when she did her last year at university here. She can't get over it – she said in Korea most city brides wear white these days in the Western tradition, she's so pleased I'm wearing it.'

Jake turned from Morgan and said to Alba's aunt, 'I didn't know what she was going to wear, but it's perfect, isn't it? She looks like a beautiful little doll - I can't believe how lucky I am to have her. Best thing that ever happened to me.'

As they continued towards the head table at the front of the room he looked down at her and asked quietly, 'Did John and Margaret say anything in particular? I was busy fending off my lawyer's effusive wife when they came up to you, so I didn't hear any of the conversation.'

'Nothing special,' said Alba. 'They just congratulated us. No strong feelings at all, so he's given up on the resentment, I think.'

'I'm not one for making speeches,' said Steve, who looked slightly uncomfortable standing behind his chair at the head table in his dark suit, handsome and serious. 'I never made one at my own wedding, and that's what I want to talk about today. History has repeated itself in an unexpected way. I married Alba's mother when she had just turned twenty-one and I was forty-one, I think. Mary and I met great opposition to our marriage from both our families, but we proved everyone wrong. We were we totally happy right up until the day Mary died, far too young and in the middle of a good career. But I'm very lucky to have a wonderful daughter, who has today married a man many years older, and I hope they will be just as happy as Mary and I were. At my wedding there were no speeches, because we were married in a registry office with only two friends as witnesses. Today I'm happy to have both sides of the family here to wish Alba and Jake well. Alba's wearing her mother's engagement ring and at the side of her hanbok she has the norigae tassel Mary wore at our wedding, and which has been in her family for generations. And now, a toast to the perfect couple!'

THANK YOU

We hope you've enjoyed reading this story and would consider leaving a review, or even a rating.

These are not only much appreciated, they also help other readers discover new authors.

For other titles from Lightpool Publishing, please read on.

ABOUT SASKIA

Saskia Woodhill is an emerging author or soft romance novels where slightly paranormal characters occasionally engage in outrageous behaviour and sometimes find themselves in funny or dangerous situations - or funny and dangerous at the same time. Stories that will make you laugh and cry and turn the pages to the satisfying ending.

OTHER TITLES FROM
LIGHTPOOL PUBLISHING

Letters from the Past by Tina Clough is a series of stand-alone novels where a letter from or about the past reveals something that changes a woman's perceptions of her family, and affects her outlook on life. Life can change in a moment and sometimes you have to step into the unknown and take a chance on love.

Having had nobody in her life since her husband died, Lara unexpectedly finds herself involved with three men. One is planning to use her, one she plans to use for her own ends, and one becomes a "friend-with-benefits" with surprising results. Sometimes a quiet schoolteacher is not all she seems at first glance.

Callista experiences an event of apparent ESP at the Okehampton Castle ruins and becomes a media sensation, but the effect it has on her life is dramatic. How do two people, one calm. one seriously claustrophobic, who feel they are poles apart, cope for an hour and a half in total darkness in a stalled lift? And can they handle the consequences?

Sofia's life is in turmoil: a difficult diva mother, a letter with a confession about a family killing and having to accept help from a man she loathes when she is injured. Can reluctant attraction turn into love?

Who is the stranger living in the empty house Miranda inherited from her grandmother? Why is he living like a secretive recluse in someone else's house? Reckless Miranda decides to confront him, and what she discovers prompts her to set out on a fearless quest to bring justice to a man who has given up hope. But is the gamble too great or a risk worth taking?

When Emma finds an old letter in a library book she is instantly intrigued, but by researching the origin of the letter she unwittingly opens the door to danger and becomes the target for threats and harassment. Nearly desperate, she takes a leap of blind faith into the unknown and accepts an offer of help from a stranger - but can she trust him?

Jamie, an ardent protester against the gigantic Vista Resort development and Leo Masters, the high-powered developer, seem unlikely to ever agree on anything. But unexpected coincidences and chance brings them together in a fragile state of mutual respect. Will courage and kindness resolve the situation, or do they need help?

After a bizarre accident with ESP overtones, the media haunt Arapera. But can she trust an offer of help from a man she has only met once? Or will she regret it for the rest of her life if she doesn't take the chance? Sometimes life is a knife-edge balance between staying safe and taking risks, and there is no way of predicting if the gamble is worth it.

When crime-writer Saskia finds an unconscious stranger, she has a strange and strong emotional connection. Pretending to be his cousin and with no thought for the consequences, she spends weeks at his hospital bedside. But what will happen when he wakes and discovers she has invaded his life, breached his privacy and made crucial decisions on his behalf?

THE GIRL WHO LIVED TWICE

What would you do if you woke up one morning and found that time had rewound exactly a year? Would you revisit your past mistakes and try to do better? Would you try to get revenge on those who had wronged you? Or would you use what you knew to get rich? When Mia finds herself in her own past, she must decide how best to use her pre-knowledge of one year's worth of events and personal issues.